P9-DMD-890

GUIDE TO THE WORLD OF FAIRIES

BY ANDREW DONKIN
ART BY GONZALO KENNY

LOS ANGELES • NEW YORK

WITH LOVE FOR FISHER, LEXIE, AND VIV.

—A.D.

For information address Disney Press, 1200 Grand Central Avenue, Glendale, California 91201.

Printed in the United States of America
First Hardcover Edition, June 2019
FAC-038091-19137
1 3 5 7 9 10 8 6 4 2

Designed by Gegham Vardanyan

Library of Congress Control Number: 2019935579

ISBN 978-1-368-04077-8

DisneyBooks.com

Logo Applies to Text Stock Only

CONTENTS

DEAR MUD PERSON:

Yes, I mean you, human. That's what we call you—Mud People. Because, well, you live in (or I suppose, on) the mud. Prepare to have your mind completely blown! This book is going to change everything you think you know about the world. And I mean everything.

Remember all those stories about elves, dwarfs, goblins, and trolls? You probably heard them from your Mud Parents when you were little and then forgot all about them. Well, guess what? They're all true. Every single one of them. Those creatures all exist right under your feet as part of a hidden fairy civilization kept secret from you. Thousands of fairies living together in underground cities full of amazing technology and fantastic food. Its very existence is classified TOP SECRET from humans.

But now, this book, *my* book, is gonna blow the lid off that secret once and for all!

An organization calling themselves the Lower Elements Police (L.E.P.) has stopped all fairy contact with Mud People for many centuries. Any non-official fairy creature that attempts to get to the surface finds themselves stopped and captured by the dreaded L.E.P. We can be imprisoned for just trying to observe a Mud Person in their natural habitat.

Well, I want to change that.

My name is Nord Diggums. I am a dwarf, and am widely regarded underground as the most handsome tunneler of my generation. By bringing this heretofore classified information to the attention of the Mud Person world, I want it to be known that I am placing myself in extreme danger of losing my freedom and spending the rest of my days in a cell in the notoriously terrible Howler's Peak Prison. I know. Pretty selfless of me, right? I'm sure you are thinking that the only suitable way for the Mud Man civilization to repay my selfless actions would be to make me the most famous, most adored, and wealthiest person on the planet. That would be nice. But, of course, it really wouldn't be my place to say.

To date, only a handful of Mud People know the truth. This book is not afraid to name names. (Or name objects, or name anything really. But I digress.) One of the people "in the know" is a juvenile criminal mastermind called Artemis Fowl, who—along with his bodyguard, Butler—enacted a plan to revive his family's fortune by kidnapping a fairy and holding her for ransom. What happened next and the exploits of L.E.P. Officer Holly Short and her boss, Commander Root, are known to the People (as we call ourselves) underground but not to humans. Yet. My hope is that with the publication of the *Guide to the World of the Fairies* stories such as theirs—and others—will be forced out onto the surface. If someone is going to make a huge fortune from exposing the existence of fairies, than surely it should be a fairy (or more specifically, a tunneling dwarf) that strikes gold.

The *Guide to the World of the Fairies* is the most comprehensive (which means full of all the facts that you want to know—I looked it up) guide to the People and their underground existence ever published.[1] I have gathered together the most extraordinary talents and commissioned articles and writings by the brightest minds, all to provide you despicable (I mean, uninformed), polluting humans with the latest lowdown on what's going down underground. (Read that sentence again. Sometimes I amaze even myself.)

ARTEMIS FOWL II

Artemis Fowl II is a Mud Child, and one to avoid at all costs. Along with his man mountain of a bodyguard, Butler, Fowl is one of the few humans on the surface to know about the existence of the People.

The most dangerous thing about Artemis Fowl is his mind. He has an exceptionally high IQ and is a self-declared criminal genius. He is particularly skilled at analyzing a situation and working out the likely outcomes. Physically, Fowl has pale skin and raven-black hair. Fowl's brain and Butler's brawn make their partnership a highly effective one. Fowl has claimed "I never tell people exactly how clever I am. They would just be too scared."

He lives in Fowl Manor, near the city of Dublin in Ireland. The Fowls are a family of criminals and do-badders who will stop at nothing to get rich. Fowl came into contact with the Fairy Folk when he plotted to kidnap L.E.P. Officer Holly Short and held her for ransom, demanding a large quantity of gold to free her. This kidnapping sent shockwaves through the Lower Elements Police and a Time Stop was rapidly put over Fowl Manor while Commander Root attempted to free Captain Holly Short. Don't worry. I know you Mud People can be sensitive. It all worked out in the end.

[1] Editor's Note: As proven by the fact that it's the ONLY guide.

HOLLY SHORT

Holly Short is a captain in the Lower Elements Police (L.E.P.). She is an elf and is around eighty years old. Holly Short started her L.E.P. career on traffic patrol in the east side of Haven City before working her way up to L.E.P.recon, the L.E.P. section that deals with rogue runaway fairies. Captain Short has proved her courage in combat situations many times, not least when taking on a rampaging troll single-handed to save a Mud Man village.

Unfortunately for her, she is best known as the fairy involved in the Artemis Fowl affair, during which she was captured by that same Mud Child. Captain Short was held hostage in the human's ancestral home as the young criminal attempted to relieve the People of a large quantity of gold. Ever since, Captain Short has spent much of her time trying to prove herself to her boss, Commander Root.

Each chapter will feature all you could possibly want to know about the different fairy species. We always start with an informative introduction written by yours truly. We then have our Spotter's Guide, a kinda lesson 101 on the basics of each fairy race. After that we have some notes "borrowed" from Fowl Manor, revealing the innermost thoughts of the Mud Child Artemis Fowl about the fairy races.[2]

Encrypted Message

These are TOP SECRET notes, and it is forbidden to remove them from the grounds of Fowl Manor. Such an occurrence will be punishable by a visit from my bodyguard.

AF II

[2] Editor's Note: The stuff from the Fowl kid is undated, so we don't know exactly when it was written.

Next up are some specially commissioned thoughts from my cousin and occasional partner-in-crime (metaphorically speaking, of course), Mulch Diggums.

HEY NORD, WHAT DO YA WANT ME TO WRITE HERE? IT'S FOR THE INTRODUCTION, RIGHT? THAT MONEY BETTER BE IN MY ACCOUNT WHEN I CHECK LATER ON. YOU KNOW I DON'T WORK FOR FREE. YOU WANT ME TO TALK ABOUT MYSELF FOR A WHILE? LADIES LOVE THAT.

MULCH

The main feature of every chapter is an article or interview written or narrated by a leading light in the field of that species.

TROLLS

What you don't know about trolls can get you killed, so start your voyage through the fairy underground by finding out about these carnivorous creatures before they can find you. Get the lowdown on the hunting habits of trolls, how to survive a troll attack, and much more from Haven City University's resident troll expert, Professor Seekem Oot.

ELVES

Elves are sometimes said to be the most magical of the fairy races. Find out about their many magical gifts, how they renew their powers, and why they make such good L.E.P. officers in an article by Haven City University anthropologist Ivana Therey.

PIXIES

Pixies occupy some of the most important positions in Haven City society. Once again, Professor Ivana Therey provides insight into this intelligent—and confident—species of fairy. She also gives you clear insight into what it's like to share an office with someone who has a larger brain than you do.

SPRITES

Professor Ivana Therey's final contribution to the book is an in-depth look at sprites. Born to fly, sprites are the happy-go-lucky free spirits of the fairy world. Don't get yourself into a flap, read about the only species of fairy with natural wings right here in this very important chapter.

GOBLINS

However hard you try, you can't live in Haven City long before coming into contact with goblins. Expert Dr. Belleva Beste explains why goblins aren't as bad as everyone thinks they are. I'll let you make up your own mind as to whether or not she's right.[3]

GNOMES

Gnomes are the craftspeople of the fairy world, but they are shy and prefer isolation to the company of others. T. J. Fleetstream, an officer from Haven City's Inclusivity & Diversity department, breaks wide open the stereotypes surrounding this ancient and powerful species. Find out about their dedication to their jobs, crafts, and falling asleep on a pile of gold here.

[3] Editor's Note: Actually, I won't really let you make up your own mind. You are a Mud Person. You've never dealt with a goblin. Dr. Beste might try her best to make them seem misunderstood, but I'll give you the truth. They are bad news. Plain and simple.

GREMLINS

The most underrated and misunderstood of the Fairy Folk. Once again, our expert, T. J. Fleetstream, explains how gremlins are just here to help. You Mud People will be happy to see some of your very own history in this chapter. Although, perhaps not happy when you see the specific topic.

DWARFS

Probably the most popular and widely loved species of fairy is the handsome and brilliant dwarf. We asked the smartest, best-looking dwarf we could find to write the stereotype-smashing article on this fantastic—and did we say handsome already?—fairy species. I was delighted to do it.

KRAKEN

Kraken are slow-moving, huge seagoing beasts, roughly the size of a small island. These gentle giants are currently under the excellent care of the Kraken Watch headed up by Captain Jac Cuztard. He writes about his three decades in Kraken Watch, just for us.[5] You'll learn what makes a kraken tick, why you should never cook lunch on one, and what to do when it's shell-shedding time. (Hint: Run!)

DEMONS

We also have the story of the "missing" fairy family, the demons. Not even fairies know the full story where demons are concerned, so, frankly, I'm hoping to shift quite a few copies of this book underground as well. This demon chapter is written by someone who claimed to have worked for a spooky organization called Section Eight and to know the secret truth behind occasional, supposed sightings of demons even though they have been gone from Earth for ten thousand years. Maybe

[5] Editor's Note: Obviously he didn't know it was for an exposé for a Mud Publisher, or he probably wouldn't have done it. There are times it's best to be economical with the truth.

he did. Maybe he didn't. I included his story and you can take it with a grain of stinkworm droppings.

CENTAURS

We've been lucky enough to nab an exclusive interview with Haven City's most famous centaur, Foaly. The L.E.P.'s backroom genius inventor talks about centaurs, ancient centaur history, why centaurs get lonely, and what it's like to have the brains of a genius and the body of a horse. Miss this gallop through centaur society and you'll be missing a rollicking good time.

FAIRY TECHNOLOGY

Lastly, but by no means leastly, we follow up the horsey thoughts of the previous chapter with a look at the amazing fairy technology of the Lower Elements Police with the man who knows it best, the L.E.P. Academy chief training officer, Paye Tention.

I hope you'll agree that all of this material, collected in one volume at considerable risk to my person, represents great value for the money—unless you are still reading it for free, in which case it represents unbelievable value for the money, and you need to put it down. I don't get paid unless the book sells, so be a pal and help me out. Like all dwarfs, I need to know there really is a light at the end of the tunnel.

Your pal,

Nord Diggums

CHAPTER 1

TROLLS

WE START OUR GUIDE TO THE WORLD OF THE FAIRY PEOPLE WITH A CHAPTER ABOUT THE MOST DANGEROUS CREATURES UNDER THE EARTH: TROLLS. THEY ARE THE MEANEST, LOUDEST, AND MOST FURIOUS ANIMALS THAT YOU ARE EVER LIKELY TO RUN INTO. BEST TO GET THE WORST OVER WITH, WHICH IS WHY TROLLS FEATURE IN OUR FIRST CHAPTER. I'M DELIGHTED TO SAY THAT OUR MAIN FEATURE ARTICLE IS WRITTEN BY PROFESSOR SEEKEM OOT, WHO HAS SPENT HIS LIFE STUDYING THE TERRIFYING CREATURES AND IS ABSOLUTELY CONSIDERED TO BE THE WORLD'S NUMBER ONE AUTHORITY ON TROLLS.[1] WE START, HOWEVER, WITH OUR SPOTTER'S GUIDE TO HELP YOU IDENTIFY TROLLS IN GENERAL.[2]

SPOTTER'S GUIDE TROLLS

SPECIES: Troll. There are over three hundred recorded subspecies of trolls, ranging from the common deep-tunnel troll to the increasingly rare smooth-skinned mole troll. New species of troll are emerging at an accelerated, magical rate.

LOOKS LIKE: A huge scary hungry monster with claws, tusks, and big sharp teeth.

SIZE: Bigger than you. Much, *much* bigger than you.

PERSONALITY: Sometimes hungry. Sometimes grumpy. Sometimes hungry *and* grumpy.

MOST LIKELY TO BE CAUGHT DOING: Something they shouldn't, like eating people.

MOST EASILY SPOTTED WHEN: They are in pursuit of a screaming mob of terrified people they want to eat. The troll will be the hungry-looking one at the back.

---

[1] Editor's Note: By me, anyway.

[2] Editor's Note: If you think you might be currently in the company of a troll, then it's possibly best to read this bit on the move. Run!

Encrypted Message

Hello, Butler.

Here, old friend, are my tactical notes on trolls. As we both know, when it comes to the Fairy People, trolls are the most physically dangerous species of them all. Even their name is a giveaway, originating from the Old Norse for "giant" or "demon."

If we ever have cause to engage a troll in another combat situation, then our lives might well depend on your ability to enact the detailed battle strategies I have worked out. (I promised I'd keep these notes focused, Butler, and I have! One of the big advantages of a genius-level mind such as mine is its phenomenal ability to stay focused on a single subject. A brilliant mind does not get distracted, as inferior minds would, by wandering off the topic to talk about side issues, which, however interesting they might be, are utterly irrelevant to the subject at hand.)

Trolls have incredible physical strength, but they also have three weaknesses, all of which we can use to our advantage in battle. First, they are by no means the most intelligent species among the Fairy People. Their brainpower is limited and their thinking speed is slow compared to a normal human. (Incredibly slow compared to me, obviously.) Their second major vulnerability is their aversion to bright lights. Trolls can cope with normal low-level lighting, but a burst of intense light at close range can efficiently incapacitate them. Third, they have a weak spot at the base of their skull. This is probably the least useful of the three, because one would have to be close enough to the troll (and its teeth) to be able to hit it. Please read my notes and we can meet in my study at four p.m. after school to discuss them.

AF II

I'M REALLY HAPPY TO TALK ABOUT ALL THE OTHER FAIRY TYPES, BUT I DO NOT WANNA TALK ABOUT TROLLS. I HATE 'EM. BUT IF I GOTTA, THEN FIRST OFF, THERE ARE TWO THINGS I HATE ABOUT TROLLS. FIRST: EVERYTHING. . . . OKAY, THERE ARE THREE THINGS I HATE ABOUT TROLLS.

FIRST: EVERYTHING.

THEN, MORE SPECIFICALLY: YOU CAN'T TRUST A TROLL ON A BANK JOB. YOU MIGHT THINK, OKAY, LET'S GET A TROLL IN ON THIS. GREAT IDEA. HE CAN BUST THROUGH A BANK WALL; HE CAN RIP THE DOOR OFF A SAFE LIKE IT WAS TISSUE PAPER; HE CAN MAKE A STENCH WITH HIS REAR END THAT WOULD RENDER ANY NIGHT-SECURITY-TYPE OPERATIVE UNCONSCIOUS IN A MATTER OF SECONDS. SO YEAH, LET'S GET A TROLL ON THE TEAM. A BIG, LUMBERING, DUMB BRUTE OF A TROLL TO BE THE MUSCLE. BUT YOU'D BE WRONG! DON'T DO IT! IN THE MIDDLE OF THE CUNNINGLY CONCEIVED AND PRECIOUSLY PLANNED BANK JOB, YOUR BIG DUMB TROLL WILL REMEMBER HE HASN'T EATEN FOR, LIKE, MAYBE FIFTEEN MINUTES AND WANDER OFF TO FIND A NICE TASTY POODLE OR NIGHT WATCHMAN TO SNACK ON. HE WON'T CARE IF HE LEAVES A HANDSOME DWARF IN DIRE TROUBLE SOMEWHERE ELSE IN THE BANK. PERHAPS THAT VERY SAME DWARF MIGHT BE SUFFOCATING IN A VACUUM-SEALED VAULT, BUT THE TROLL WON'T CARE IF HIS HUGE TROLL TUMMY NEEDS FILLING!

THE OTHER REASON I HATE TROLLS IS THAT TROLLS ARE DISGUSTING. THEY ARE DIRTY, SMELLY, AND UNHYGIENIC. THEY ARE THE MOST PHYSICALLY FOUL ANIMALS UNDER THE EARTH. I STILL CANNOT BELIEVE THAT SALLY SHORESITE DUMPED ME TO GO OUT WITH ONE. DUMPED ME, MULCH DIGGUMS, FOR A TROLL! (I SAY "DUMPED," ALTHOUGH WE WEREN'T TECHNICALLY GOING OUT, BECAUSE I HADN'T GOT UP THE COURAGE TO SPEAK TO HER YET, BUT IT WAS ONLY A MATTER OF TIME BEFORE SHE BECAME AWARE OF ME AS PRIME BOYFRIEND MATERIAL. THEN THAT TROLL COMES ALONG AND RUINS EVERYTHING.) THAT'S WHY I DO NOT WANNA TALK ABOUT TROLLS. I HATE 'EM.

MULCH DIGGUMS

AFTER ATTENDING HAVEN CITY UNIVERSITY TO STUDY ZOO-TROLLOGY, PROFESSOR **SEEKEM OOT**, A PIXIE, MADE HIS FIRST TRIP TO OBSERVE TROLLS IN THEIR NATURAL HABITAT. HE DESCRIBES THE EXPERIENCE OF SEEING THE BLOODTHIRSTY CARNIVORES UP CLOSE THUSLY: "A REVELATION OF THE SPLENDOR OF THE NATURAL WORLD FROM WHICH I HAVE NEVER RECOVERED." FILMING HIS AWARD-WINNING DIGITAL SERIES *TROLL PLANET*[3] TOOK OVER THREE AND A HALF YEARS AND INVOLVED THE AUTHOR AND TECH CREW TRAVELING AND FILMING IN OVER ONE HUNDRED THOUSAND MILES OF DEEP TUNNELS. HIS NEW WORK, *LIFE UNDER EARTH*, IS TOUCHINGLY DEDICATED TO HIS THREE STAFF MEMBERS WHO WERE EATEN WHILE RESEARCHING THE BOOK.

MY LIFE WITH TROLLS

By Professor SEEKEM OOT

For me, one of the most magnificent sights in all of nature is an adult troll on the hunt. This is evolution's most perfect predator.

Daily life for a troll is both simple and brutal.[4] Their behavior is governed almost entirely by the overwhelming desire to feed. With a height of nine to twelve feet for a fully grown adult and a weight of up to 550 pounds, a troll spends much of its waking day searching for the huge amount of food it needs to survive.

Today, trolls dwell almost exclusively in the deep tunnels of the underground, encouraged by the L.E.P. to stay away from the bright lights and tempting cooking smells of our own Haven City. If a troll does wander toward Haven City suburbia, it is quickly driven by the L.E.P. forces back to where it can do no harm to the fairy citizens of our dear city.

[3] Editor's Note: Did you catch it on FFC? Great show.

[4] Editor's Note: Sounds like my first marriage.

OF TROLLS AND TUNNELS

Finding enough food to survive in the tunnels can be tough (which is why trolls do occasionally venture to the surface). They have an acute sense of smell; they can sniff out food at a distance of over five miles. But hunting down that food can take time, especially if said food is on the move. There also may be other trolls on the hunt for it, meaning that time is of the essence.

There's an old saying that trolls will eat anything as long as it's still alive, and by and large that is true. Trolls are fierce carnivores and their diet consists of

LOOKS INNOCENT, RIGHT? DON'T BE FOOLED. THIS IS A COMMON TUNNEL TROLL, CAUGHT MOMENTS BEFORE HUNGER OVERCAME HIM AND HE DESTROYED AN ENTIRE SUBWAY SYSTEM.

whatever meat they can get their claws on. Cats, dogs, cows, dwarfs, brilliant academic staff with a bright future of discovery ahead of them—trolls do not mind what they eat.

They much prefer their meat to be as fresh as possible, but if hungry enough, they have been known to scavenge someone else's kill. Trolls will hunt as a pack or as individuals, depending on the species of troll and its environment. It's well-known that trolls will fight each other for food, although serious injuries are rare unless both trolls are starving. After a show of bluster, it is typical for the smaller troll to back down in the hope of having a meal of leftovers in due course. During times of hardship, when food is scarce, packs have been known to turn cannibal, consuming the weakest, slowest-moving, or most tasty-looking member of the group.

During a long hunt, trolls have been witnessed slipping into a kind of blood-lust state. In this condition, the troll is utterly crazed while hunting its prey, even to the point of overlooking obvious physical dangers to itself. During one such episode, a troll in pursuit of an L.E.P. officer attached itself to the outside of the L.E.P. pod as it was blasted into a magma flow. The troll did not trouble the L.E.P. officer again.

On rare occasions, one of these creatures will find its way, by accident or design, up to the surface world. A troll's journey to the world of Mud People is nearly always a long and exhausting trip through a labyrinth of twisting tunnels. It's not surprising, then, that when they emerge onto the surface, they do so half-crazy with hunger.

A troll that has reached the surface will usually be disoriented and confused, its simple troll mind trying to make sense of its new surroundings. As much as trolls love food, they have a hatred of bright lights that is far greater. The human world is a confusing combination of easily available food items (pizzas, cows, dogs, people) and a never-ending assault of bright lights.

A troll on the surface is the L.E.P.'s worst nightmare, and it is easy to understand why. A glimpse of an elf in the dark woods can be readily dismissed as the workings of an overactive Mud Man's imagination. A huge troll-sized hole through the side wall of a human dwelling is a little harder to explain away, and would risk alerting the Mud People to the existence of us all.

AS WELL AS UNFORTUNATE ANIMALS AND PEOPLE, TROLLS CAN ALSO FEED ON THE RESIDUE ENERGIES THAT CAN BE FOUND AT MANY OF THE PLANET'S MAGICAL HOTSPOTS. I BET A COW IS TASTIER THOUGH.

There is one infamous incident describing how a troll residing under a bridge was tricked by three above-average-intelligence billy goats, all of whom, the reports claim, were named Gruff. The first two Billy Goats Gruff tried to cross the bridge but were stopped by the snarling troll, who threatened to eat them. They tricked their way across the bridge by suggesting the hungry beast wait for their plumper and much tastier older brother. Licking his lips, the troll agreed. When the third and oldest Billy Goat Gruff crossed the bridge, he charged at the troll and knocked the ravenous creature into the river, where he was carried away by the current. This is generally thought to be the all-time number one most popular bedtime story among goats ever.

Interestingly, trolls are so frightening that even Mud People have legends and myths about them. Before Fairy Folk gave up the surface to the Mud Men, trolls made their homes in caves, tunnels, and, sometimes, in the shadowy hollows underneath bridges built by primitive Mud Men. This close proximity gave rise to sightings and sightings gave rise to stories.

CLOSE ENCOUNTERS OF THE TROLL KIND

I will always remember my first real-life encounter with trolls. I was a student in the early days of my zoo-trollogy degree program and on my very first field trip. It's hard to pick out individual moments, but I'll try. I recall the red flashes of anger in their eyes, the musky smell of their blood-matted fur, and the screams of my fellow academics as we fled for our lives. The sound of ripping tent fabric still gives me nightmares.

Around a dozen students and lecturers from the zoo-trollogy department were on an end-of-term field trip to the derelict Eighth Wonder Theme Park. As anyone with an interest in trolls knows, this long-abandoned theme park has been overrun by trolls for many decades. Our field trip leader, Dr. Wight Fishlicker, had hoped that we would be able to observe a troll pack from afar and perhaps even make contact with them at some point. Unfortunately, they had very much the same idea, though their idea was perhaps not as scientific in nature. They attacked us while we slept. There was blood, screaming, and absolute terror. I've never seen trolls look so happy. Most of our party escaped, and the ones who didn't are remembered every year in a special section of our Graduation Day ceremonies.

This incident raises the controversial question of the intelligence of trolls. The traditional image of a troll is of a dim-witted beast driven only by its instinct to feed. While we have seen that they are indeed driven by their stomachs, they have at times shown unnerving ingenuity to get their meals. Trolls have been seen setting simple traps to ensnare unwary victims, both animal and fairy. Some authorities claim that their intelligence is superior to "any common snail or goldfish," and the evidence gathered in my long career indeed bears this out.

THERE'S NO BUSINESS LIKE TROLL BUSINESS

There are examples on record of trolls learning things and working with other species. That sounds unbelievable today, but the ancient elfin parchments of Borris the Blagger tell us it's quite true. As recently as a few hundred years ago, troll sideshows still toured Haven City and Atlantis, setting up their tents and playing the large crowds of delighted onlookers. The last recorded legal troll sideshow was performed by the infamous Count Amos Moonbeam, a troll that would belch out a version of "The Ballad of Tingly Smalls" in exchange for being drip-fed honey punch by its dwarf handler, Maxmo the Sticky.

Not all these shows were quite what they seemed, though. History tells us that some of these troll sideshows actually featured two dwarfs standing on each other's shoulders and wearing a long hairy coat while relieving the cheering crowds of their money before quickly escaping.

Trolls haven't just been used in show business. Back in our ancient past, before the Fairy Folk were driven underground by the advancing tribes of Mud Men, trolls were used in battle as part of the fairy army. The Sacred Scrolls of Gladfly the Annoying record trolls charging into battle, being ridden by dwarfs. These combinations were referred to as Troll Riders. The Troll and dwarf worked together as a mighty force on any battlefield. It's thought that the troll received instructions from its rider via yanks on its braids, sending it this way to batter an enemy or that way to crush a foe. We can only imagine the terror the Mud People in the opposing forces must have felt when seeing a row of Troll Riders emerging from the mists across a battle zone and charging straight at them. During the course of my zoo-trollogy research, I have had the pleasure of interviewing many of Haven City's oldest citizens about these battles, compiling a firsthand-witness archive that is second to none in the academic world.

Life for trolls today is a far cry from the way it was when some of them served in the fairy army. Today, as much as I might wish it were otherwise, trolls live a life as outcasts from fairy society.[5] They live, feed, breed, and die in the wild deep tunnels that surround Haven City.

THE MODERN TROLL

In a modern troll pack, structure is based purely on physical strength. Whichever troll can bite the hardest and bellow the loudest will become the alpha troll. The

A MALE TROLL IN THE MIDST OF WHAT WE BELIEVE IS A DEFENSIVE DANCE MARKING HIS TERRITORY. UNFORTUNATELY, NO ONE HAS EVER BEEN ABLE TO GET CLOSE ENOUGH TO REALLY FIND OUT THE TRUE MEANING OF THE DANCE OR IF IT IS COMMON TO ALL TROLLS OR JUST THIS BEAUTY.

[5] Editor's Note: I think you're alone in that wish, buddy!

alpha troll can be replaced at any time, and there is usually a waiting list of young pretenders to the throne.

Trolls mostly communicate with each other through nonverbal "signals" that include punches, whacks, kicks, pushes, and thumps. There are claims that some trolls have been able to learn certain simple elements of sign language, but this is not usual, and in my years of study, I have not personally witnessed such a thing. Not entirely unknown, but much less common, are reports of trolls being able to speak or at least grunt actual simple words. Whether this is true language or just copycat sound-making is yet unknown.

The holy acorn of zoo-trollogy research has to be to teach a troll to be fluent in sign language, to enable it to communicate freely and so allow us to learn more about their life cycle. Two main obstacles have prevented this from happening so far: first, due to the recent belt-tightening of the pixie banking sector, there is a lack of funding resources within the Haven City university sector; and second, everyone who has attempted to teach sign language to a troll has been eaten alive.[6]

TROLLS—ACCESS ALL AREAS

In terms of territory, trolls exhibit very different behaviors depending on their breed and circumstances. Some trolls are very territorial and will spend centuries living in the same cave or under the same bridge. In some extreme cases, the troll will remain in its territory long after the food supply has dwindled or even vanished. In stark contrast, other trolls spend the majority of their lives on the move, living as nomads.

The L.E.P.'s troll division has multiple witness statements describing a particularly well-traveled troll known as Suspect Zero or Gruff. Believed to be one of the oldest trolls in the world, Suspect Zero has traveled the globe, visiting magical hot spots. Trolls feed on the magical residue in such locations. This energy nourishes them and prolongs their lives. Suspect Zero is likely responsible for multiple sightings of what Mud Men call the Abominable Snowman and Bigfoot.

Readers should be aware (in every sense) that there are many different species of troll all over the planet. Despite their lack of intelligence or

[6] Editor's Note: Ouch!

complex society, trolls have proven themselves to be one of the most enduring and adaptable of the Fairy People. Many of them have evolved to fill a particular niche in their biosphere, giving rise to a startling variety of adaptations. Here are four examples that illustrate the amazing adaptability of trolls as a species.

AMAZON HEEL-CLAW TROLL—This tropical troll lives in crevices and caves within the Amazon basin. The thick jungle canopy means that many areas are shaded and protected from the sun, perfect for the light-hating trolls. The Amazon Heel-Claw has a reputation as a silent killer that lies in wait for its victims to pass, then suddenly grabs them. Luckily, even the most amateur troll observers can easily spot its distinctive clawed heel. Little is currently known about this shy and silent species, but I'm soon setting out on another research trip that I hope will shed light (metaphorically, of course) on the Amazon Heel-Claw troll.

THE HEEL THAT GIVES THE AMAZON HEEL-CLAW ITS NAME. YEAH, AS IF TROLLS WEREN'T FRIGHTENING ENOUGH.

ANTARCTIC BLUE—Proving just how adaptable trolls are, the mighty Antarctic Blue is at the other end of the temperature scale. Adapted for life (if you can call it that; there are no libraries or coffee bars) on the planet's coldest continent, the Antarctic Blue spends most of its time underground in the warmer vents beneath the permanent snow cover. Antarctic Blues are noted for their huge size. It's highly likely that evolving in such a cold biosphere has slowed down the creatures' natural metabolism, allowing them to live longer and therefore grow larger. It would be fascinating to get a DNA sample to find out exactly how long these solitary creatures live, but so far no one has been brave enough to try.

RIDGEBACK—This is a more common species, found particularly in caves in mountainous areas. Its distinguishing feature is its distinctive comb of thick spiked hair that runs from its brow to its tailbone. Its fur is an unusual blue-tinged gray. Ridgebacks are one of the least aggressive troll species, as long as they are not rubbed the wrong way.

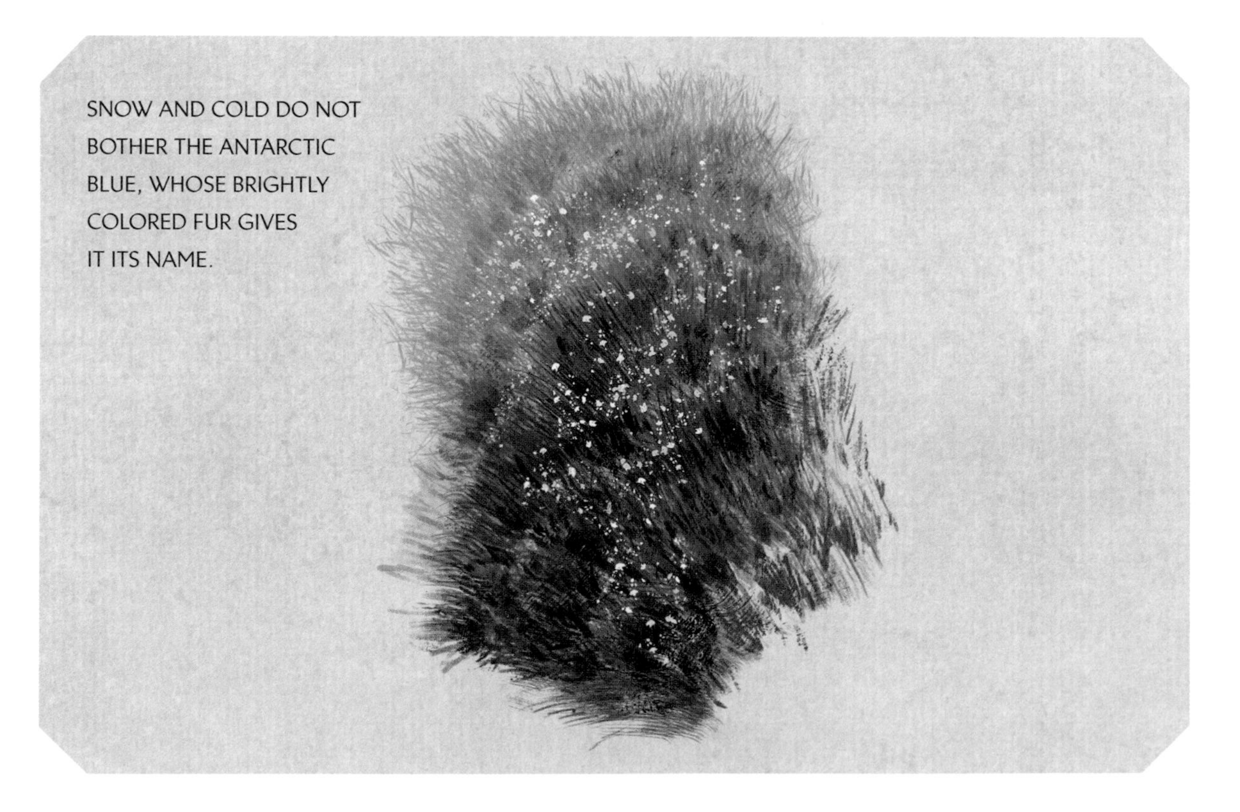

SNOW AND COLD DO NOT BOTHER THE ANTARCTIC BLUE, WHOSE BRIGHTLY COLORED FUR GIVES IT ITS NAME.

SIGHTINGS OF THIS PARTICULAR SPECIES OF TROLL OFTEN CAUSE SEVERE FEAR IN THE ONLOOKER. IT IS IRONIC AS THE RIDGEBACK IS ACTUALLY RATHER KIND AND NON-AGGRESSIVE . . . AS FAR AS TROLLS GO.

ORANGE VENT—The Orange Vent troll—or, more correctly, the Orange Vent Hard-Shelled troll—is one of the most elusive creatures under the ground. Believed to live only near hot magma vents, these trolls have evolved so that their already tough hair has matted together to form heat-resistant shells resembling organic body armor. Because of the difficulties in observing these creatures, little is known about their lives except that they must be hot. Really hot.

A FINAL WORD:

I have spent my entire adult life studying trolls. They are the most fascinating, varied, and—let us be honest—hungry creatures. If the above article has piqued your interest, then why not consider joining our excellent zoo-trollogy department at Haven City University, either as a student or as a member of the staff? Due to a number of unfortunate troll-related incidents, we currently have several vacancies.

ELVES

HAVING ESCAPED FROM THE TROLLS IN OUR FIRST CHAPTER, WE NOW TURN OUR ATTENTION TO THAT MAINSTAY OF HAVEN CITY SOCIETY . . . ELVES. ELVES MAKE UP AROUND 30 PERCENT OF THE POPULATION OF OUR GREAT UNDERGROUND METROPOLIS, INCLUDING A FAIR NUMBER OF OFFICERS IN THE LOWER ELEMENTS POLICE.[1] ELVES ARE THE MOST MAGICAL OF THE FAIRY RACES. THE AVERAGE ELF ASSIGNS GREAT IMPORTANCE TO KEEPING HIS OR HER MAGICAL ABILITIES UP TO SCRATCH. TO GIVE US THE FULL LOWDOWN ON ELVES (AND LATER PIXIES AND SPRITES), WE ASKED SOCIAL ANTHROPOLOGIST IVANA THEREY FOR HER TAKE ON ELVES, THEIR MAGIC, AND THEIR PLACE IN FAIRY SOCIETY. WE START WITH OUR SPOTTER'S GUIDE . . .

SPOTTER'S GUIDE — ELVES

SPECIES: Elves

LOOKS LIKE: Typically have pointy ears but there is variety of skin and hair colors.

SIZE: Elves stand a little over three feet tall.

PERSONALITY: Elves are intelligent, loyal, and have a very strong sense of right and wrong.

MOST LIKELY TO BE CAUGHT DOING: Something in the Lower Elements Police to bring lawbreakers to justice and protect the citizens of Haven City.

MOST EASILY SPOTTED WHEN: They are bringing a suspect into custody. They are the usually the smaller, happy-looking fairy who is not in cuffs.

[1] Editor's Note: That's my guess anyway. Who knows the real number. Count them yourself if you're that bothered.

Encrypted Message

Butler:

As you know, we have had more direct contact with elves than any other species of the People. Both the impressive Commander Root and our one-time guest at Fowl Manor Holly Short are elves. During our close encounter, they seemed smart, skilled, and highly professional. Kidnapping Short turned out to be even more dangerous than we had anticipated. Even with my huge intellect, in the end we were lucky to escape with our lives.

We have much to learn if we are to get the better of them during future adventures. We must study their magical abilities as well as their technology and we must tease out the weaknesses in both.

AF II

What can I say? Some of my best friends are elves. Well, one of my best friends is an elf. Of course I'm talking about Holly Short, of the L.E.P. It might seem strange that a dwarf such as my handsome self could be pals with someone whose job it is to uphold the law, but I guess it just goes to show the strength of my personality.

Holly is no pushover, and ain't that the truth, but she is (and I can't believe I'm actually saying this) just about the fairest L.E.P. officer that you could ever hope to get arrested by. I understand if her deep friendship with me is something that she would find embarrassing if revealed to her fellow officers. Let's just hope they never get to read this, eh. :)

Mulch

IVANA THEREY IS A SOCIAL ANTHROPOLOGIST FROM HAVEN CITY UNIVERSITY. SHE IS AN ACKNOWLEDGED EXPERT ON THE LIVES OF ELVES, PIXIES, AND SPRITES. HERE WE ASKED HER TO GIVE US A BRIEF INSIGHT INTO THE LIVES AND POWERS OF ELVES.

MORE TO THE UNIFORM

By Professor IVANA THEREY

ELVES

Elves make up the largest share of the population in Haven City, holding many jobs and playing many roles in the city's great institutions. Elves are, by and large, intelligent and loyal, and they get on very well with all the other fairy races.[2]

Elves are considered the most magical of the Fairy People and magic certainly plays an important part in their daily lives.

THE RITUAL

Like most Fairy People, elves must renew their magic when it runs low by performing the Ritual. The classic Ritual involves a journey to the surface when there is a full moon in the sky. The moon does not have to be full to complete the Ritual, but it is preferred, as less magic is absorbed if the Ritual is completed under anything but a full moon.

To perform the Ritual, the elf recharging his or her magic must take an acorn from an ancient oak tree and perform a brief ceremony that involves burying it in fresh earth while reciting the words "I return you to the earth,

[2] Editor's Note: As do we dwarfs, of course. We get on with absolutely everyone except goblins. And maybe gnomes when they take our gold. And pixies when they're being snooty. And sprites when they're doing all that show-offy flying stuff. And elves because they're all such Goody Two-shoes. Apart from them we love everybody.

AN ELF PERFORMING THE RITUAL UNDER THE BRIGHT LIGHT OF A FULL MOON. A TRULY MAGICAL EXPERIENCE. THE RITUAL RESTORES A FAIRY'S MAGICAL POWERS AND ALSO FILLS THEM WITH A SENSE OF DEEP JOY AND CONNECTION TO THE EARTH. (SO THEY TELL ME.)

and claim the gift that is my right." If the fairy recharging their magic is injured at the time, their wounds will usually be healed immediately by the act.

It is a beautiful thing to watch a fellow fairy complete the Ritual. Such moments are typically private affairs for most fairies, so often only family and very close friends share in it. As the incantation is spoken, a burst of colorful magic rises from the ground and cascades into the fairy's body. As it does so, it recharges every single magical cell.

Many elves also report that after performing the Ritual, they feel better and more powerful, and have a renewed sense of purpose in their lives. At this point, the elf is at the peak of their magical powers and is said to be "running hot," meaning they are packed with magic.

DANGERS OF THE RITUAL

Having to perform the Ritual under moonlight means that an elf has to undertake a pilgrimage to the surface in order to complete the ceremony that will renew their magical powers. Not only does this involve a lot of paperwork to get the needed permission, it also means risking being spotted by a Mud Person.

The L.E.P.'s resident tech genius, the centaur Foaly, turned his mind to the issue. His first invention to try and solve the problem was a Sealed Acorn Unit that contained a previously harvested acorn. The unit was designed to be carried by L.E.P. officers to give them the option of a quick emergency recharge if they didn't otherwise have access to an acorn. However, this innovation was rejected by the Fairy Council as heresy.[3]

Never one to give up, Foaly went back to the problem and created a new invention—Lunar Panels. This device collects moonlight on the surface and pipes it underground, all the while retaining the moonlight's magical frequency. The stored moonlight is then shone out of a fake moon orb suspended from the cavern's roof high above Haven City, giving exactly the same magical effect as direct moonlight above on the surface. Foaly's underground moon orb follows the cycle of the real moon perfectly.

This was a revolutionary life-changing event for elves and all the

[3] Editor's Note: Which is typical of the slow-moving old-fashioned numties.

other magical creatures in Haven City who perform the Ritual, giving them a way of renewing their magic while remaining safely underground.[4]

ELVES & THE LOWER ELEMENTS POLICE

Many elves serve the city as members of the green-uniformed Lower Elements Police. Stand by the entrance to L.E.P. Headquarters in Police Plaza and you will see elves aplenty displaying what dedicated public servants they are.[5]

The Lower Elements Police consists of several different sections of which elves are valued members:

TRAFFIC DIVISION—the usual starting point for newly qualified recruits.

STREET PATROL—officers on city-wide patrol.

AERIAL UNIT—largely made up of sprites although elves can be recruited.

IMMIGRATION—paper-pushing department that handles visas for legal and sanctioned visits to the surface.

INTERNAL AFFAIRS—the department that deals with policing the police.

AN ELF IN A TYPICAL L.E.P. UNIFORM. AS COMMON AS ACORNS ON THE FORCE.

[4] Editor's Note: And you can bet your last credit that Foaly hasn't stopped going on about it ever since.

[5] Editor's Note: Ugh! Just the thought of standing outside L.E.P. Headquarters for the day sends an icy blast of fear down my beautiful dwarf spine. Not for any particular reason, of course. No reason at all why I should fear that institution bent on catching criminals.

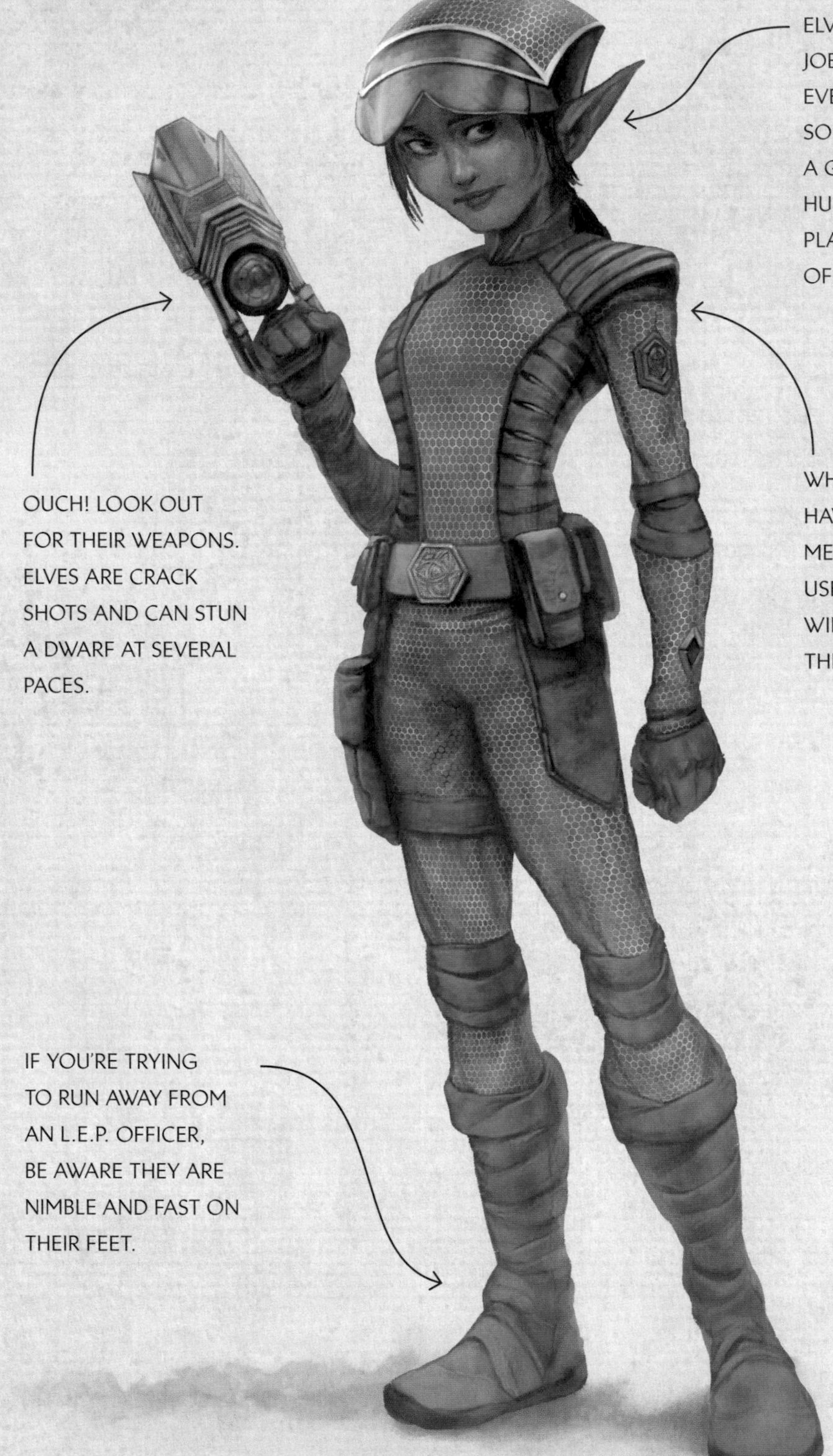

ELVES TAKE THEIR L.E.P. JOBS SERIOUSLY, BUT EVEN I GOTTA ADMIT SOME OF THEM HAVE A GOOD SENSE OF HUMOR. NOTE THE PLAYFUL LOOK IN THIS OFFICER'S EYE.

WHILE ELVES DO NOT HAVE NATURAL WINGS, MEMBERS OF THE L.E.P. USE MECHANICAL WINGS TO TAKE TO THE SKIES.

OUCH! LOOK OUT FOR THEIR WEAPONS. ELVES ARE CRACK SHOTS AND CAN STUN A DWARF AT SEVERAL PACES.

IF YOU'RE TRYING TO RUN AWAY FROM AN L.E.P. OFFICER, BE AWARE THEY ARE NIMBLE AND FAST ON THEIR FEET.

KRAKEN WATCH—a small department that monitors the mostly dormant kraken population in the world's oceans.

L.E.P.RECON—an elite branch that deals with runaway fairies, trolls, and anyone else making illegal trips to the surface.[6]

L.E.P.RETRIEVAL—after L.E.P.recon has located the runaway fairy, this department removes them and clears up the mess.

MISSION TO THE UNKNOWN

The most dangerous territory for any L.E.P. officer to navigate is not the deep tunnels and the dangers of trolls and other wild beasts that live there. No, the most dangerous area is the surface world, where a single mistake by just one fairy or L.E.P. officer could result in the Mud People discovering the existence of the People. That is why the work of the L.E.P.recon department is so vital in catching runaway or rogue fairies BEFORE they can be spotted or captured by Mud People. All fairies owe the L.E.P.recon squad a debt of continued thanks.

Any surface mission begins with the pre-op check known as "The three Ws," which refers to Wings, Weapons, and a Way home. Unlike sprites, who have natural wings, elves have no wings and can fly only with the aid of mechanical sets provided by the L.E.P.[7]

If an elf, or any fairy for that matter, takes the pre-op check seriously, it drastically increases their chances of making it to—and back from—the surface safely and without incident. Even if just one of the Ws is not checked off, it could spell disaster—for all of fairy kind.

ANCIENT WISDOM

Like all fairies, elves are governed by the laws and wisdom recorded in *The Booke of the People*. Created by King Frond (see sidebar on page 28), *The Booke* is a collection of all the laws, secrets, wisdom, and traditions that fairies must follow. It is what governs how they live their lives. Frond was wise enough to put in place a worldwide spell such that if a copy of *The Booke* is touched without the owner's permission, then it bursts into flames. The spell (along

[6] Editor's Note: Everyone knows "L.E.P.recon" is where the Mud People get their word "leprechaun" from. Honestly. I'm too kind to my readers.

[7] Editor's Note: Don't take her word for it—see our chapter on fairy technology. Don't skip to it now—you'll spoil the ending!

with Frond's famously short temper) earned him the nickname Frond the Easily Combustible.

Some verisons of *The Booke* are able to morph and take on several physical shapes. It can appear as a large, heavily decorated silver book, or alternatively small and round and about the size of a matchbook. The text inside is written in an ancient and rather difficult form of Gnommish. One of the first lessons fairy children learn in their Oak Grade classrooms across Haven City is how to translate pages of *The Booke* into modern oral form.

HEALING

Elves are masters of the healing arts. The healing power usually manifests itself as a cascade of blue sparks that works its way from the hands of the healing elf into, and through, the body that's being healed, until eventually the power is drawn to the parts that need to be repaired.

If a magically charged elf themselves is injured, then they will automatically begin to heal without the elf even needing to be conscious for it to happen. This auto-healing has saved the lives of many elves over the centuries. Healing powers

KING FROND

King Frond, also known as Frond the Easily Combustible, was an elf and the first king of the united People. Frond led them against the Mud People ten thousand years ago at the Battle of Taillte.

He was responsible for, back then, setting into place what are considered today to be the social norms of fairy society. He drew together ancient wisdoms and a startling variety of magical texts to create *The Booke of the People*. He also had his powerful warlock council create the Rule of Dwelling. The introduction of the Rule of Dwelling was extremely controversial at the time, and Frond only just survived an attempted plot to overthrow his royal rule by his half brother, Dodd the Duffer.

EXCERPT FROM THE *BOOKE*

THE BOOKE OF THE PEOPLE

Being instructions to our magicks and life rules[8]

Carry me always, carry me well.
I am thy teacher of thy herb and spell.
I am thy link to power arcane.
Forget me and thy magick shall wane.

Ten times ten commandments there be.
They will answer every mystery.
Curses, cures, and alchemy;
These secrets shall be thine through me.

But, Fairy, remember this above all:
I am not for those in mud that crawl,
And forever doomed shall be the one
Who betrays my secrets one by one.

[8] Editor's Note: the spelling is correct. Some of the words are ye olde.

BEFORE KING FROND WROTE *THE BOOKE* AND SET FORTH LAWS TO FOLLOW, THE FAIRY WORLD WAS WILDER AND HARSHER. HERE, TWO YOUNG ELVES ARE ON THE RUN. WHY? WE WILL NEVER KNOW.

HERE, AN ELF HEALS HIS FELLOW OFFICER WHO HAS BEEN INJURED IN THE LINE OF DUTY. SHE WILL WAKE, HEALED AND NONE THE WORSE FOR WEAR. PRETTY HANDY WHEN YOU MAKE YOUR LIVING KEEPING THE LAW.

can also be used to attach some smaller body parts that may have become separated, like fingers or ears.[9]

In some limited circumstances, elf healing powers may be capable of bringing someone back from the dead if healing is attempted very quickly after the fatal injury. In cases where the injuries are very serious and the elf's powers are not enough by themselves, it's been known for the healing spell to drain energy from the person's own life force. Thus the victim awakes healed but perhaps a decade or two older than they were before the time of the accident. Arguably that's a price worth paying if the injury would otherwise have proved fatal.

The process of magical healing involves the replication of healthy cells to replace those cells that are damaged or dead. Any impurities (such as a bullet or shrapnel) are likely to get replicated as well, which could cause health issues in the future.

NOTE: Injuries that are serious or complicated should be referred to a qualified warlock medic. **DO NOT ATTEMPT TO HEAL THE NEARLY DEAD AT HOME.**

EVERY LITTLE THING SHE DOES IS MAGIC

Many accidents in Haven City go unreported because they are solved by a dose of elfin healing magic at the scene, saving the injured person a hospital trip. All on-the-spot healings (or OTSHs as they are called) should be included in the officer's crime or accident report. It is an enormous advantage for the city to have so many elves with this ability serving as L.E.P. officers on patrol.

If a lot of healing energy is required, then the elf healer may need to rest afterward to regain their strength. L.E.P. regulations state that any officer involved in a healing that lasts more than twenty seconds needs to end their shift and report back to headquarters for mandatory R&R.

An elf's healing ability is not limited to just other fairies. As far as we know, their healing magic works across all species. There are numerous records from the ancient times of elves healing a Mud Person in exchange for something that the elf wanted, such as food or water or a human baby to look after for a couple of centures. More recently, it has been reported that L.E.P. Captain

[9] Editor's Note: Ouch!

Holly Short healed several humans during her encounters on the surface.[10]

MESMER

All elves have the ability to use mesmer, which is the ability to magically hypnotize a human. To successfully use mesmer, the eyes of the elf must be in direct line of sight with the eyes of the subject. It's been shown, at great cost, that mirrored reflective sunglasses (through which the elf cannot see the wearer's eyes) prevent the mesmer from working. There have also on occasion been some strong-willed Mud People who have been able to fight the effects of the mesmer.[11]

When mesmerized, the subject is open to suggestion, be that instructions to action or answering questions with total honestly. Mud People have described the voice they hear while being mesmered as like that of a choir singing in perfect harmony. Sometimes after a Mud Person has been under the effect of mesmer, their eyes will look tired or even bloodshot.

It is against Fairy Law to ever use a mesmer on a fellow fairy, and such an

A YOUNG ELF GIRL LEARNING THE MAGIC OF MESMER FROM HER PARENTS. THE GLYPHS ON THE WALLS HELP TO CHANNEL MAGICAL ENERGY AND INCREASE THE EFFECTS OF THE MESMER.

---

[10] Editor's Note: I think we know who you mean!

[11] Editor's Note: Not naming names, but we all know we are referring to a certain mountain-sized bodyguard.

act would have severe consequences. Over the centuries, the ability to mesmerize Mud People has proven useful when a fairy has been surprised by a human on the surface.

BY INVITATION ONLY

Like all fairies, elves lose their magic if they enter the dwelling of a Mud Person uninvited. For an elf to lose his or her magic is a tragic thing, and most go to any lengths to avoid it. If a fairy *does* enter a human dwelling without an invitation, either on purpose or by accident, they will quickly suffer dizziness and sickness, and eventually (if they stay) lose their magical powers forever.

There is evidence that the Rule of Dwelling has been weakening over the passing centuries. In fact, this development has led to debate among the Fairy Council and L.E.P. officers as to the possibility of removing the spell in order to better serve investigations.

HOLDING YOUR TONGUE

Another magical power that elves share with most other fairies is the Gift of Tongues. Simply stated, this means elves can understand, and be understood in, all languages. This doesn't just apply to the many hundreds of Mud People languages that pollute the surface of our planet, but also to many animal languages such as dog, cat, dolphin, and squid. The Gift of Tongues requires a sizable amount of magical energy and as a result, many fairies prefer to operate a digital translator if dealing with other languages for long periods of time.

THE MORE THE MERRIER

While we are used to seeing the common elf species in Haven City, there are other species that have adapted to live and thrive in entirely different environments.

AMAZONIAN ELF—Suited to life in tropical temperatures, Amazonian Elves are fast on their feet and have a distinctive yellow arrowhead pattern on their skin to resemble flowers.

EUROPEAN TREE ELF—Most Haven City elves are descended from the European Tree Elf also known as the common elf.

DOUBLE-EARED ELF—The distinctive mark of the Double-Eared Elf is, of course, the double point or peak found on their tip of their ears. Most Double-Eared elves now reside in Atlantis.

SILVER FOX ELF—This subspecies of elf resides in more northern climbs scattered around the edge of the arctic circle. They are identified by their beautiful and lush silver hair. Silver fox elves are known for their ability to charm almost any being they come into contact with.

WEB-TOED ELF—Most common along coasts and swamp areas. Web-toed elves do not have gills and cannot breathe underwater, but thanks to their obvious adapted extremities, are as fast in water as they are on land.

CHAMELIO ELF—The Chamelio Elf has evolved to use its magic to render itself nearly invisible by matching whatever it is standing in front of or even near. Because this requires massive amounts of magic, chamelio elves have no other magical powers. It is thought that the Chamelio Elf is now extinct, although frankly, as they are practically invisible, it's rather hard to tell.

ELF AND SAFETY

There's no doubt that the whole of the Fairy People owe elves a debt of thanks for their magical help in keeping Haven City running. Whether on the L.E.P. or simply offering their healing abilities out of the kindness of their little elf hearts, elves have, and continue to, keep our fairy civilization safe.

CHAPTER 3

PIXIES

AFTER ELVES, WE HAVE TO TALK ABOUT PIXIES. THEY LOOK A LOT LIKE ELVES (AT LEAST TO US DWARFS) BUT DON'T EVER GET THEM MIXED UP!

THE PIXIE POPULATION OF HAVEN CITY NUMBERS LESS THAN ELVES, BUT THANKS TO THEIR TALENTS AND BRAINPOWER, PIXIES HAVE HAD A HUGE IMPACT ON OUR CITY. PIXIES ARE BUSINESSPEOPLE, SCIENTISTS, DOCTORS, PROFESSORS, AND L.E.P. OFFICERS. IN OUR MAIN ARTICLE, IVANA THEREY CONTINUES HER LOOK AT HAVEN CITY SOCIETY.

SPOTTER'S GUIDE PIXIES

SPECIES: Pixies

LOOKS LIKE: Of all the fairy races, pixies are the ones that most resemble Mud People. The most visible difference is their size and their pointy ears.

SIZE: Pixies stand about two and a half feet tall.

PERSONALITY: Many pixies are extremely intelligent. Most are ambitious in terms of their careers and earning potential. However, like all species, there are a few rotten apples in the bunch. Some pixies have a reputation for being greedy and generally lacking morals.

MOST LIKELY TO BE CAUGHT DOING: Anything that gets them ahead in life.

MOST EASILY SPOTTED WHEN: They get the promotion you didn't.

Encrypted Message

Butler:

I'm deeply fascinated, Butler. *The Booke of the People* talks about pixies as being the most intelligent of the Fairy Folk. Could a pixie match even my brainpower? It's hard for me to imagine that anyone, whatever their species, could ever be my intellectual equal, let alone best me mentally. (Although to be fair I must admit that so far elves and trolls have given us a good run for our money already.) But a pixie with a combination of high intelligence and low morals might be just the kind of business partner we need. (Maybe?)

AF II

If you ever wanna feel inferior, go on a blind date with a pixie. Especially the deputy head of production at Koboi Chemical Plants. That was the worst blind date I ever had. I don't know what my cousin was thinking setting me up like that.[1]

Firstly, the East Bank is all granite and I was wearing my best clothes that I didn't wanna mess up, so I decided to walk there instead of tunneling. Long story short? I end up getting chased through the alleys of East Bank by a goblin gang with blasters who thought there was nothing funnier than taking potshots at a dwarf looking for romance. So I got to my date fourteen minutes late (not fifteen as was claimed) with a few blaster impact marks on my new suit, and it basically went downhill from there.

Moral of the story? If you are a dwarf looking for romance, DO NOT go on a blind date with the deputy head of production at Koboi Chemical Plants. I know that's pretty specific advice, but it's solid. Trust me.

Mulch

[1] Editor's Note: Not me, another cousin. Honest.

IVANA THEREY IS A SOCIAL ANTHROPOLOGIST FROM HAVEN CITY UNIVERSITY. SHE IS AN ACKNOWLEDGED EXPERT ON THE LIVES OF ELVES, PIXIES, AND SPRITES. HERE WE ASKED HER TO GIVE US A BRIEF INSIGHT INTO THE LIVES AND POWERS OF PIXIES.

NOT JUST PRETTY FACES

By Professor IVANA THEREY

PIXIES

Where elves and pixies differ is that the latter much more closely resemble miniature Mud People. Pixies are the only fairy species that could convincingly pass for a human. Pixies have slightly enlarged heads compared with elves and sprites, and this gives them a strange childlike appearance and a look of innocence.

Pixies are among the most talented and intelligent of the People. They are physically skilled at sports like running and excel as inventors and academics. Pixies have a large brain contained in skulls of unusual thinness, a combination that makes the species prone to more brain-related conditions and diseases than either elves or sprites.

While pixies do possess some fairy magic, in general their connection to it is much weaker than most elves. Because pixies do not like being second best at anything, most pixies give up using magic to concentrate their talents in other areas.

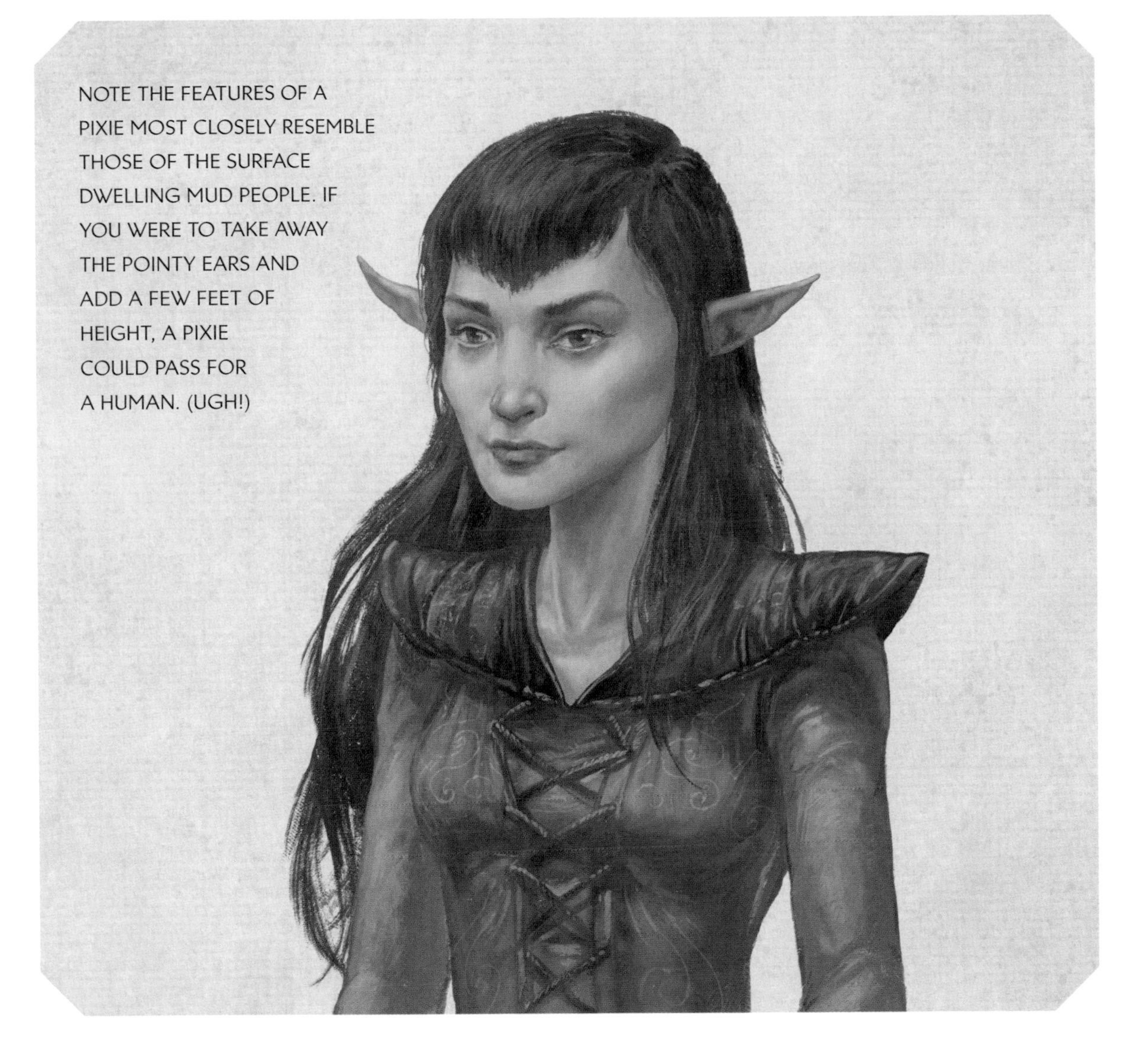
NOTE THE FEATURES OF A PIXIE MOST CLOSELY RESEMBLE THOSE OF THE SURFACE DWELLING MUD PEOPLE. IF YOU WERE TO TAKE AWAY THE POINTY EARS AND ADD A FEW FEET OF HEIGHT, A PIXIE COULD PASS FOR A HUMAN. (UGH!)

I have to be circumspect in what I say as I'm an elf myself, but pixies are universally known for their wide-ranging ambition.[2] If you've ever been at school with a pixie you will know how much they hate not coming top in any classroom test. To come in second place in the school sports day

[2] Editor's Note: Listen, she's not wrong. She's actually being way too kind. However, I can say what I like, and it's a fact that pixies are greedy, they have few, if any, morals, and they will do nearly anything to get what they want. As a dwarf I have absolutely nothing against pixies, but that's the truth of it.

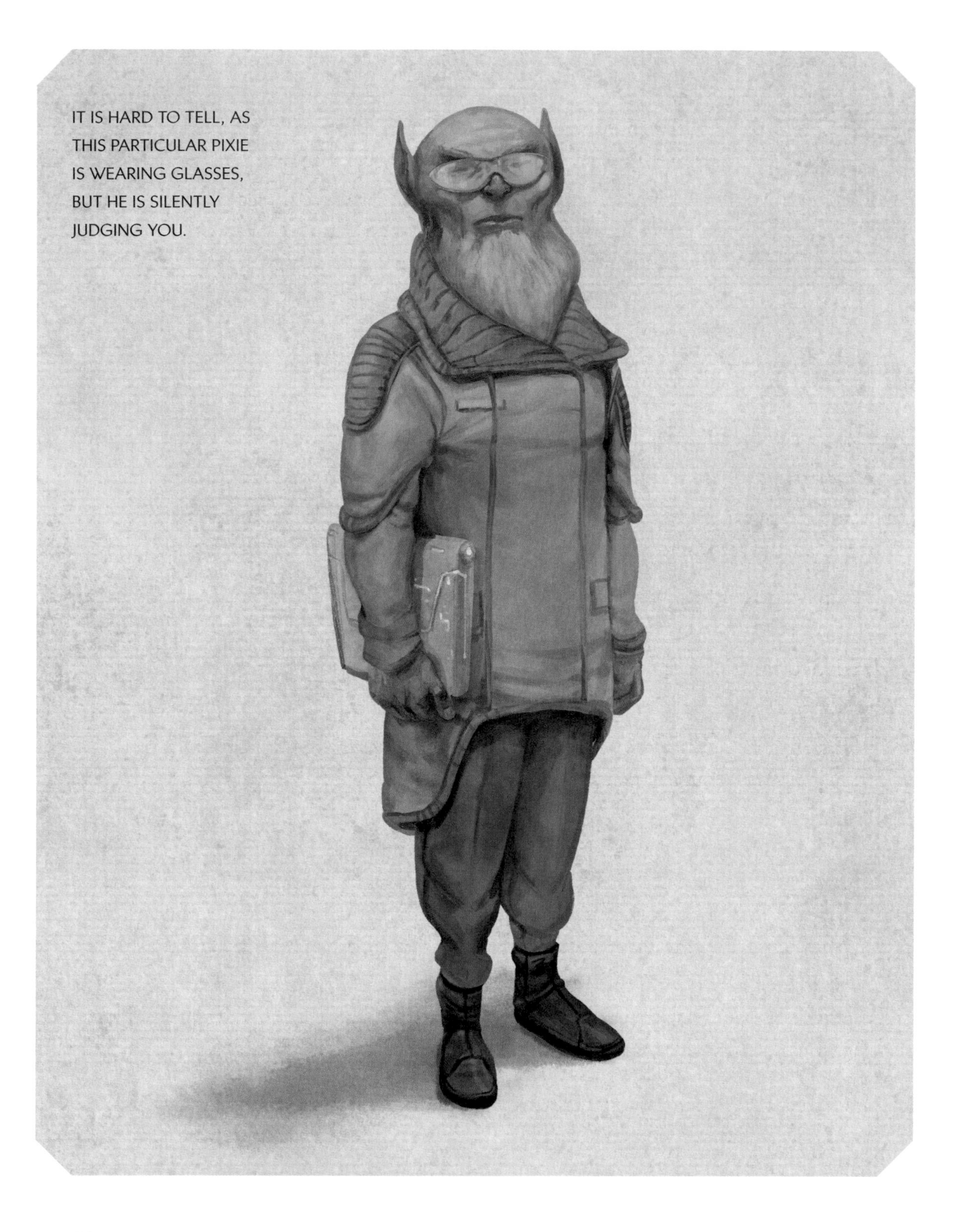
IT IS HARD TO TELL, AS THIS PARTICULAR PIXIE IS WEARING GLASSES, BUT HE IS SILENTLY JUDGING YOU.

spoon-and-stinkworm race would cause any pixie almost physical pain.

The fact that pixies are so ambitious doesn't mean that they all hold the top jobs, though. If there's one thing a pixie loves more than getting a promotion themselves, it is seeing a fellow pixie *not* get a promotion. The Haven City Department of Commerce estimates that in any given office or workplace over 7.5 percent of work hours are spent by one pixie trying to drag down their fellow pixies.

Pixies tend to have very firm views about what they like and what they don't like, and this includes food. Pixies will sometimes stick to eating exactly the same meal for month after month until they eventually tire of it and it is replaced by another favorite. Many pixies have a real fondness for shellfish, which is, of course, illegal. This has led to the blossoming of a huge underground (well, it would have to be) black market dealing in the smuggling of lobsters and other outlawed creatures that it is forbidden to eat due to Haven City rules on protected species.[3]

SUBSPECIES

There are a few subspecies of pixie that are worth mentioning:

JUMBO—Larger-than-normal pixies born in the underwater city of Atlantis. It's believed that the increased pressure is the cause of their increased girth. They are said to be rather primitive and resemble Cro-Magnon Mud People.

ATLANTEAN BLUE—A rare breed of pixie from Atlantis. As the name suggests, this subspecies has skin and eyes that are aquamarine blue.

WINTER GRAYS—In the ancient times these were high-altitude pixies who lived in caves and tunnels in mountain ranges. Haven City pixies say they haven't heard from them in ages, but then, pixies were never great at keeping in touch.

SAY HI TO HYBRIDS

When talking about elves and pixies it is worth noting that a union between the two species produces a hybrid, or crossbreed, known as a pixel. Hybrids are always one of a kind, even when

[3] Editor's Note: If you're a pixie and you're reading this, then firstly, let me apologize for my previous remarks about pixies. Secondly if you want to score some fresh lobster via a certain shellfish smuggling legend whose surname is Day, then get in touch. I'm here for you. We can do a deal. Call me. This is real.

L.E.P. OFFICER LAZULI HEITZ ON A TRAINING MANEUVER FLIGHT OVER A SAFE ZONE. WE CAN CLEARLY SEE THE CHARACTERISTICS INHERITED FROM BOTH SIDES OF HER FAMILY TREE. THE LONG BLOND HAIR IS FROM HER AMAZONIAN ELF PARENTAGE WHILE HER BLUE SKIN REMINDS US OF AN ATLANTEAN PIXIE, THE OTHER SIDE OF HER DNA HERITAGE.

NOTE THE PATTERNS OF YELLOW ARROWHEAD MARKINGS WHICH ARE TYPICAL OF AMAZONIAN ELVES. IT'S BELIEVED THESE MARKINGS EVOLVED SO THE AMAZONIAN ELVES RESEMBLED SUNFLOWERS TO AIRBORNE PREDATORS.

the combination of parent species has been combined before. Hybrids often do not have the magical powers of their parent species, but may well have other abilities that make up for that. L.E.P. Officer Lazuli Heitz is a pixel who combines the blue skin of an Atlantean pixie with the blond hair of the Amazonian elf. Mottled over her naturally blue skin are the yellow arrowhead markings that once made Amazonian elves look like sunflowers to airborne predators.

SURPRISING TURNS

While pixies may be limited in number, they have proven time and time again that might does not make right. Pixies continue to surprise us as they take on new roles within our community that are surprisingly selfless. More and more are becoming members of the medical field where they use their intellect to help save lives and have even been known to take research roles to help discover cures for illnesses that can infect the fairy population. While some might say that they do this for the glory that such breakthroughs bring them, others argue that it demonstrates that pixies are adapting (albeit slowly) to life underground, which requires collaboration.

We hope to see pixies take on even more challenges and put themselves in positions where they can benefit all fairies, not just themselves.[4]

[4] Editor's Note: Pixie Power! Seriously, if any of you pixies need shellfish, give me a call.

SPRITES

I NEVER MET A SPRITE WHO DIDN'T LIVE TO FLY. IT'S ALL THEY THINK ABOUT AND ALL THEY WANT TO DO. I GUESS YOU WOULD, TOO, IF YOU WERE BORN WITH AMAZING NATURAL WINGS THAT MEANT YOU COULD FLY. WHEN THEY HOOK UP WITH A PARTNER, THEY JUST WANT TO FLY TOGETHER. WHEN THEY START A FAMILY, THEY CAN'T WAIT TO TEACH THE LITTLE ONES TO FLY. IN MANY WAYS, THEY ARE THE MOST STRAIGHTFORWARD OF ALL THE FAIRY FOLK. IF THEY ARE FLYING, THEN THEY'RE HAPPY. OUR LAST ARTICLE FROM IVANA THEREY OF HAVEN CITY UNIVERSITY TRIES TO DESCRIBE THE JOY OF BEING A SPRITE. FIRST, OF COURSE, IS OUR SPOTTER'S GUIDE. (SPOILERS—LOOK UP!)

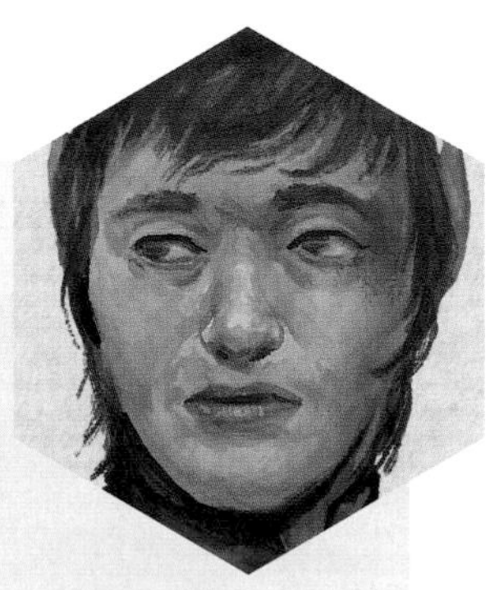

SPOTTER'S GUIDE SPRITES

SPECIES: Sprites

LOOKS LIKE: The most distinguishing feature of any sprite is the powerful pair of wings on their back. These wings are natural and are the source of pride and joy to any sprite. Sprites have pointy ears like elves and pixies, but the wings are the dead giveaway.

SIZE: About three feet tall.

PERSONALITY: Sprites are usually happy, carefree, and full of confidence.

MOST LIKELY TO BE CAUGHT DOING: Loop after loop in the air above you.

MOST EASILY SPOTTED WHEN: See above. (It really is all about the flying with sprites.)

Encrypted Message

Butler:

I wonder what it is like to fly. I don't mean in a helicopter; I know you're a qualified pilot. I mean with a pair of natural wings. That's what sprites can do and I must admit that even I'm a little amazed by it. We've experienced other fairy "gifts" close at hand ourselves (hand me the mirrored sunglasses, please) but imagine being able to soar into the sky under your own power? I imagine I can, with time, figure out my own way to fly like a sprite.

AF II

I like a guy with an interest. You know, someone who has a genuine enthusiasm for something. It might be taking part in tunneling races or it might be collecting rare and beautiful gemstones that belong to other people. I believe, and my bottom will agree with me on this, that it's very important to be an enthusiast in life. If you love something, then go for it, and that's certainly what sprites do. When I see a sprite member of the Flying Squad passing overhead with a big smile on his or her face, then I kinda can't help smiling, too. (Mainly cos it means he's missed me and I can get on with the job at hand, if you take my meaning.) Sprites, who doesn't love 'em?

IVANA THEREY IS A SOCIAL ANTHROPOLOGIST FROM HAVEN CITY UNIVERSITY. SHE IS AN ACKNOWLEDGED EXPERT ON THE LIVES OF ELVES, PIXIES, AND SPRITES. HERE WE ASKED HER TO GIVE US A BRIEF INSIGHT INTO A SPRITE'S LIFE ON THE WING.

WINGING IT

By Professor IVANA THEREY

SPRITES

Sprites are the only species of fairy to have the ability to fly using their own incredible wings. Many elves and pixies love to fly using a pair of strap-on mechanical wings, but sprites have the real thing.[1]

COME FLY WITH ME

Most of a sprite's magic is dedicated to defying gravity and flying. Scant little is left for, say, healing. A sprite can typically heal small wounds or stem a nosebleed, but for more serious injuries, an elf healer would be a much better bet. Easily the biggest organ on a sprite is his or her wings, and any injury to a wing is always serious and can sometimes be fatal.

I've never met a sprite who didn't prefer to be flying than doing anything else. They are happy-go-lucky People with a positive self-confident spin on life. They make loyal friends and good-natured employees.

Many sprites serve in the Lower Elements Police, where they are a natural fit for roles that involve flying—like traffic patrol, street patrol, and,

[1] Editor's Note: And boy, are they proud of it.

A TYPICAL SPRITE IN STANDARD L.E.P. GEAR. THE WINGS, WHILE APPEARING FRAGILE, ARE STRONG AND RESILIENT.

FLYING OVER HAVEN CITY, THIS MEMBER OF THE FLYING SQUAD IS SMILING DESPITE THE DANGERS SHE FACES. OF COURSE SHE IS, SHE'S FLYING.

of course, rapid-response teams like the famous and much-feared Flying Squad.

LET'S GET IT SPRITE

There are a few subspecies of sprites. The most common are:

WATER SPRITES—mostly based in and around Atlantis. They have large wings that when underwater resemble huge stingrays, propelling their owner through the water very quickly. Water sprites also have gills on either side of their necks that allow them to extract oxygen from the oceans and therefore breathe underwater.

AMAZON TREE SPRITES—smaller-than-usual sprites, with wings that are adapted for gliding from tree to tree rather than true flying. They are skilled at moving silently through the upper levels of the rain forest.

SPRAY SPRITES—so called because Spray sprites used to nest in caves and tunnels in coastal cliffs overlooking the sea. Their wings are adapted to coping with the powerful gusts of wind that occur near the ocean.

SWAMP SPRITES—adapted to survive in semi-aquatic environments where they use their wings to both fly

SPRITES CAN FLY UNDER THEIR OWN POWER AND TEND TO BE PRETTY ADVENTUROUS ABOUT WHERE THEY FLY, TOO. SITTING AND RELAXING OVER A SHEER THOUSAND-FOOT DROP IS NOTHING TO A SPRITE.

ATLANTIS

Atlantis is the second-largest city (after Haven City) to exist underground (or in this case, underwater). The city is contained within a huge transparent dome and is located in deep, deep water away from the prying eyes of Mud People. Its population is around ten thousand, many of whom have adapted in unique ways to survive in their underwater environment.

The Atlantis we know today is actually the second Atlantis. The first was destroyed over eight thousand years ago, after an asteroid fatally damaged the city's dome.

Atlantis is home to the Deeps Maximum Security Prison, which houses some of the People's most dangerous criminals. The prison uniform is a bright lime-green jumpsuit and is widely believed among the criminal underclass to be the most tasteless prison uniform ever created.

and swim, moving effortlessly between air and water. Swamp sprites are suspicious of their city cousins and rarely visit. They usually blame it on the city environment and the high price of soda pop from street vendors.

WE ARE FAMILY

The fairy races of elves, pixies, and sprites have more things in common than things that divide them. All are small humanoid fairies and all possess magic to some degree. It is a testament to their sense of fairy brotherhood that they live together so well in Haven City and Atlantis and beyond. Elves, pixies, and sprites have all had to come to terms with missing the surface world after the great move underground. All of them are united in their desire to dig deep and endure. As a professional who has studied all three species for centuries, this makes me feel very proud of my fellow fairy.[2]

[2] Editor's Note: * SNIFF * Pass me a hankie, I'm in tears here.

CHAPTER 5

GOBLINS

IF YOU HAVE LIVED YOUR LIFE WITHOUT EVER ENCOUNTERING A GOBLIN, THEN YOU HAVE BEEN EXTREMELY LUCKY, IN MY OPINION. MOST PEOPLE WOULD AGREE THAT HOWEVER YOU LOOK AT IT, A GOBLIN IS A HANDFUL OF TROUBLE. THIS CHAPTER PROVIDES ALL THE INFORMATION YOU NEED TO COPE WITH A GOBLIN ENCOUNTER.

ONE PERSON WHO *WOULDN'T* AGREE THAT GOBLINS ARE ALWAYS TROUBLE IS DR. BELLEVA BESTE, WHO PROVIDES OUR FEATURE ARTICLE. HER PRO-GOBLIN VIEWS ARE CONTROVERSIAL, BUT SHE WORKS CHEAP, AND THAT'S GOOD ENOUGH FOR ME.[1]

SPOTTER'S GUIDE GOBLINS

SPECIES: Goblin. There are approximately twenty-three acknowledged subspecies of goblins.

LOOKS LIKE: A green humanoid reptile.

SIZE: A fully grown goblin is a little under three feet tall.

PERSONALITY: Goblins love an argument or a fight, especially if they think they can win.

MOST LIKELY TO BE CAUGHT DOING: Time inside Howler's Peak Prison.

MOST EASILY SPOTTED WHEN: Throwing a fireball in a public place like Police Plaza.

[1] Editor's Note: Just don't take any notice of what she says.

Encrypted Message

Hello, Butler.

I've had a very interesting morning reading the new files. I am beginning to think that the Fairy Folk called goblins might be of interest to us. They seem to be, for the most part, greedy, egotistical, undersized criminals who have zero respect for any law. I find myself fond of these little miscreants. I can't think why.

Goblins might well be the perfect partners for a future caper. I've hacked some L.E.P. files that contain detailed descriptions of goblin gangs committing crimes throughout Haven City. Each gang has its own territory. Reports suggest intergang warfare is frequent and brutal. Sounds like they would be a real menace if they ever started working together, say, under a genius criminal supervisor.

I have prepared a dossier on everything I've learned about goblins. A few physical features of note: They are just under three feet tall and have green scaly skin they shed like a snake as they grow. Facially, they have large expressive eyes and a long, forked tongue set in a wide mouth. Even more extraordinary, they are able to create fireballs out of thin air. Fascinating, really.

Please read the dossier and let me have your professional opinion at your leisure.

AF II

IF THERE'S ONE THING I HATE MORE THAN TROLLS, IT'S GOBLINS. UGH! UNLESS YOU'VE BEEN LIVING IN A CAVE FOR THE LAST FEW CENTURIES—IN FACT, ESPECIALLY IF YOU'VE BEEN LIVING IN A CAVE—THEN YOU'LL KNOW THAT DWARFS AND GOBLINS AIN'T EXACTLY BEST BUDDIES.[2]

IT'S EASY TO SEE WHY DWARFS DON'T LIKE GOBLINS. GOBLINS ARE SMELLY, REPULSIVE CREATURES WHO ARE ALWAYS IN TROUBLE WITH THE LAW. THEY ARE SO COMPLETELY DIFFERENT FROM US DWARFS THAT MAYBE IT'S WHY WE DON'T GET ALONG.

RECENTLY, THERE HAVE BEEN SEVERAL FLARE-UPS OF THE GOBLIN/DWARF TURF WAR. ESPECIALLY SINCE THOSE TROLLS TOOK OVER TUNNEL E41. AS A STRICTLY IMPARTIAL OBSERVER WHO ISN'T ON EITHER SIDE WHATSOEVER, I HAVE TO SAY THAT IT'S 100 PERCENT THE FAULT OF THE GOBLINS.[3]

GOBLINS DIDN'T USE TO BE SO DIFFICULT UNTIL THE THREE "GENERALS" GOT THE GOBLIN GANGS ORGANIZED. THAT SAID, AT LEAST HALF THE ENERGY OF ANY GOBLIN IS STILL SPENT PLOTTING AGAINST AND FIGHTING HIS FELLOW GOBLINS, SO THAT SHOULD KEEP 'EM BUSY FOR A WHILE, I GUESS.

IT'S A CRUEL TRICK OF NATURE THAT GOBLINS HAVE EVOLVED AN ABILITY TO CREATE FIREBALLS OUT OF THIN AIR. ALL THEY HAVE TO DO IS CLENCH A FIST AND THINK HARD AND A LITTLE BALL OF PURE FLAME IS CONJURED INTO EXISTENCE. JUST THE IDEA OF IT SENDS A TUNNEL CHILL RIGHT UP MY SPINE. NOT, I MUST STRESS, BECAUSE US DWARFS ARE SCARED OR TOTALLY FREAKED OUT BY FIRE AND NAKED FLAMES. WE'RE NOT. WE ARE VERY CALM AND COOL ABOUT INFERNOS IN GENERAL AND, IN FACT, COULDN'T CARE LESS IF THERE WAS A HUGE FIRE RIGHT NEXT TO US.[4] CLEAR? GOOD. ANYWAY, I HATE GOBLINS.

MULCH

[2] Editor's Note: Tell me about it!

[3] Editor's Note: As a fellow dwarf, I have to say . . . he's right.

[4] Editor's Note: Again, he's correct. We dwarfs are very brave around fire. (Don't think about fire. Don't think about fire. STOP THINKING ABOUT FIRE!)

DR. BELLEVA BESTE HAS BEEN DEPUTY DIRECTOR OF THE GOBLIN CORRECTIONAL FACILITY AT HOWLER'S PEAK PRISON FOR THE LAST DECADE AND IS REGARDED AS A LEADING EXPERT IN THE FIELD OF GOBLINS AND GOBLIN GANGS. HER PHD PAPER "SHEDDING SKINS: A NEW LOOK AT GOBLINS" WON THE PRESTIGIOUS GOLDEN FIREBALL AWARD.

THE GOOD GOBLIN

By Dr. BELLEVA BESTE

Goblins often get the blame for things they have absolutely nothing to do with.

There, I've said it. It might be an unpopular opinion, but it is the truth. In a recent poll, Haven City residents were asked the following question:

How much crime in Haven City do you think is committed by goblins and goblin gangs?

On average, people guessed that 79 percent of crime in Haven City was goblin-related. In fact, the real figure is much, *much* lower.[5]

My name is Belleva Beste, and for most of my distinguished career, I have worked in the Goblin Correctional Facility at Howler's Peak. I suspect the very name Howler's Peak was designed to strike fear into the heart of anyone even thinking of committing a crime.

[5] Editor's Note: The actual figure is 77 percent.

The Goblin Correctional Facility was set up with the explicit purpose of educating goblins, in the hopes of preventing them from returning to a life of crime after their release. It has a success rate of nearly 3 percent.[6]

Most Fairy Folk think they know all there is to know about goblins, even if they have never met one. The reality, however, is often very different, and these misconceptions are what, in my opinion, have helped fuel the unnecessarily negative view of goblins. With that in mind, here is a brief Goblin 101 to help separate fact from fiction.

UNDER THE SKIN

Goblins are reptilian in appearance and are cold-blooded creatures, but whether they are true reptiles is something even the experts cannot agree on. While some like to believe goblins are larger than life, a fully grown adult is never more than three feet tall. *All* adult goblins have the ability to create fireballs at will. Exactly how much fire and energy can be produced varies from goblin to goblin.

Goblins shed their skin at regular intervals when their bones and internal organs have outgrown their current skin.[7] This occurs in two stages. First, over time, a goblin's skin will gradually turn pale green and then lose its color completely, becoming a dull gray. At this point, the next stage—the actual shedding process—will begin. This is an intensely private moment for all goblins. Within a matter of a few hours, the old skin will have fallen away or been removed, revealing the new bright green skin underneath.

The discarded skin of a wise and revered goblin leader can become, to the goblin community, a semireligious relic. This is especially true if the skin has been removed almost in one piece. It may be stuffed with discarded flakes of skin shed from lesser members of the tribe and sewn together to create a lifelike duplicate of the leader. This "doppelgänger" is then used in goblin tribal ceremonies, where it is believed to double the leader's wisdom and power.[8]

---

[6] Editor's Note: The actual figure is 2.5 percent.

[7] Editor's Note: Yeah, not their brains, I'll bet.

[8] Editor's Note: What a wacko idea that is!

GOBLINS CAN GENERATE FIREBALLS AT WILL, POSSIBLY HELPING THEIR COLD-BLOODIED BODIES KEEP WARM.

THE GANG'S ALL HERE

The structure of a goblin gang is as complex as the scaly creatures themselves.[9] Often the only members visible to Haven City residents are the trios of youthful goblins moving around the streets, but there is, in fact, an intricate hierarchy that is unknown to most outsiders. Different roles include:

HATCHLINGS—Young goblins who act as foot soldiers. Typically this occurs before their first skin shedding.

YOUNGIES—The most visible goblins on the street.

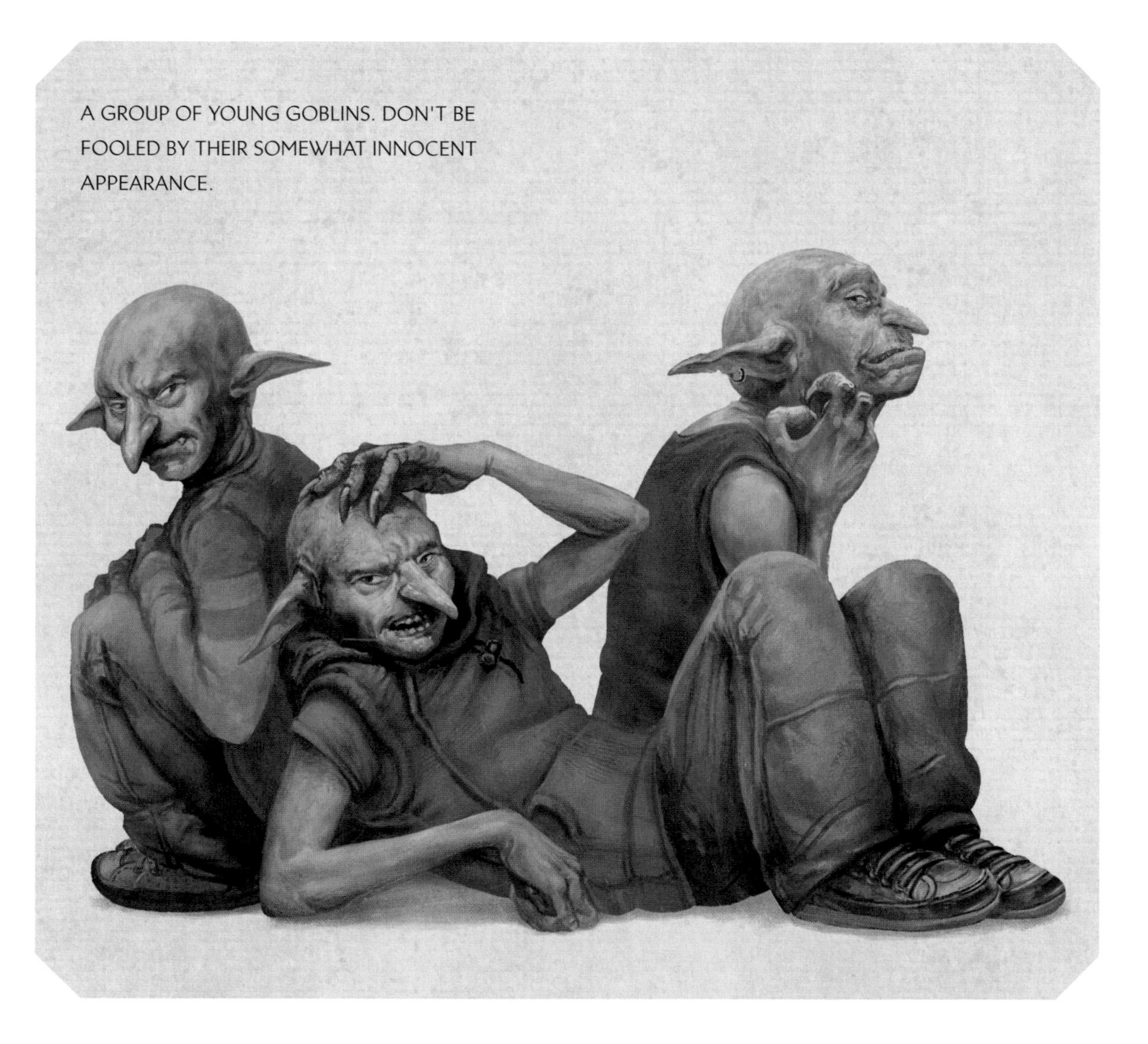

A GROUP OF YOUNG GOBLINS. DON'T BE FOOLED BY THEIR SOMEWHAT INNOCENT APPEARANCE.

[9] Editor's Note: So you mean pretty simple, then?!

SECOND-SKINNERS—Experienced street goblins.

DARK GREENS—Respected older goblins in charge of the night-to-night activity of street gangs.

GENERALS—These make up the top of the goblin food chain. This is where the real power lies.

Recently there has been an exciting development in the structure of the goblin gangs.[10] The three most powerful generals have come together to form the B'wa Kell Triad. This initiative has given the goblin gangs a more formal structure, while also greatly reducing goblin-on-goblin firefights on the streets.

The three generals in the Triad are General Sputa, General Phlebum, and, of course, General Scalene. It's very hard to get reliable intelligence on the power balance within the Triad, but what information there is indicates that it is General Scalene who calls the shots.

General Scalene is one of the best-known and most misunderstood figures in Haven City.[11] For the record, he has told me himself that he is NOT the goblin behind Haven City's organized crime syndicates. He is a deeply committed family man and often claims to have "over one thousand nephews."[12]

General Scalene owns many assets, including the Second Skin Nightclub, which is famous within goblin society as *the* place to see and to be seen. There is a strict no-fireballs rule in the ground- and first-floor bars.

It is rumored that it was General Scalene who gave rise to the "Free Our Brothers" graffiti campaign that has sprung up across the city, demanding the release of many goblin prisoners who are being unjustly held at Howler's Peak. This is the first time that goblins have been involved in a political campaign. It's a development that we will watch with some interest.[13]

GOBLIN TOWN

Goblins can be seen all over Haven City, but the greatest concentration lives in Goblin Town. Goblin Town is a maze of narrow, twisting alleys that cut across and intersect with one another.

[10] Editor's Note: Surely you mean "dangerous"?

[11] Editor's Note: Feared. Definitely feared. No misunderstanding there.

[12] Editor's Note: His Christmas-present list must be huge.

[13] Editor's Note: Concern. Watch with some concern!

There are street names posted, but it's long been said that these are regularly swapped around at random to confuse any L.E.P. personnel that might come snooping. The two wider center streets contain dozens of shops and trading posts. It's here on a warm evening that you will find the good folk of Goblin Town socializing peacefully.[14] The area is famous for its clothes and, in particular, its street-food vendors.

Goblins love their food, and their diet varies according to their social class and gang status. They are omnivores in the truest sense of the word. Goblins will eat anything. There have been

In this chapter we (or should I say Dr. Beste) have mostly considered the common or urban goblin. There are, however, another twenty-two subspecies of goblins that may be encountered within Haven City and beyond. A few of the more common subspecies are:

NIGHT-EARED GOBLIN—smaller than a normal goblin, with enormous ears. They have incredible hearing powers and are sometimes hired by goblin gangs to act as listen-outs.

THREE-EYED GOBLIN—not actually three-eyed, but the dark markings in the middle of the forehead give the appearance of a third eyeball. These are by and large shy and reclusive creatures.

HOBLIN GOBLIN—so called because extra bones on its heels give it a jerky motion as it walks or runs. To upset or make a hoblin goblin angry is considered the worst form of bad luck in goblin society.

BLACK-EYED GOBLIN—has perhaps the most startling appearance of all the subspecies, with its completely black irises. Black-eyed goblins were revered as sacred creatures by some elfin religious sects in Haven City. No black-eyed goblins have been seen in Haven City for over a hundred years. The last reported sighting was during the notorious "Hamburg Incident."

[14] Editor's Note: If you do see this, then please get a photo for me. I want photographic evidence.

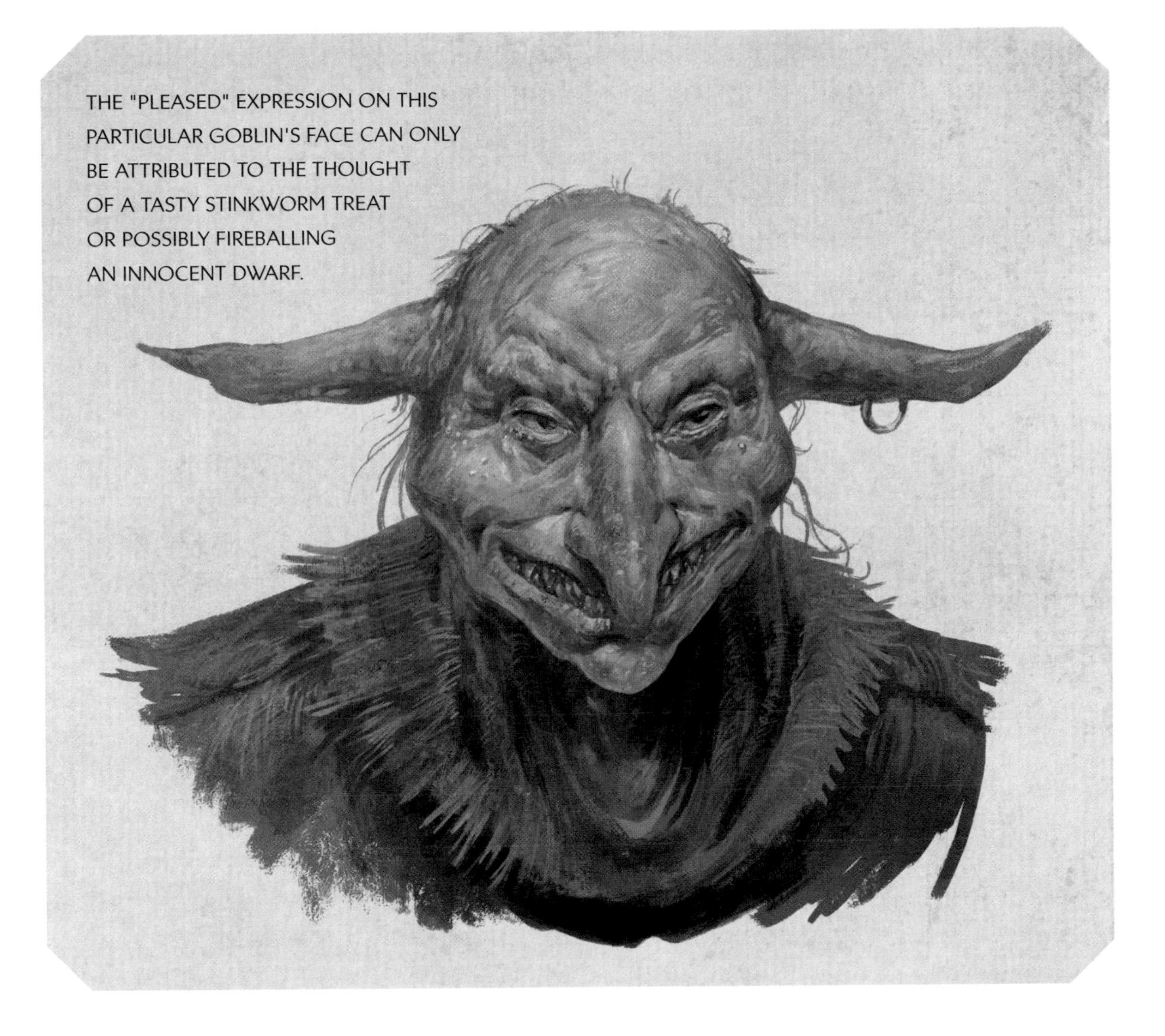

THE "PLEASED" EXPRESSION ON THIS PARTICULAR GOBLIN'S FACE CAN ONLY BE ATTRIBUTED TO THE THOUGHT OF A TASTY STINKWORM TREAT OR POSSIBLY FIREBALLING AN INNOCENT DWARF.

reports in the *Haven City Post* about goblins who have turned cannibal and consumed others of their kind. These are nothing but sensational stories designed to sell newspapers and have little basis in fact. Goblins only turn cannibal in extreme circumstances, such as if they haven't eaten for a few hours.

Goblins of every shape and creed love to eat stinkworms. While some other more sensitive Fairy Folk might pass over the chance to eat a creature cooked in its own earwax, the delicious flavors of the stinkworm are a favorite with all goblins. Goblin chefs are always trying new ways to cook the multi-eared creatures. One of the most sought-after dishes on the goblin food scene at the moment is a bowl of stir-fried stinkworm ears. As readers will know, the body of a stinkworm is covered in hundreds of ears, each one containing the earwax that gives stinkworms their unique flavor. The ears are sliced from the stinkworm, coated in flour, and then fried for just a few seconds at a very high temperature. At the Goblin Correctional Facility, we are always looking for new ways to motivate our guests (a nicer term than "prisoners") and, of late, this delicacy is used as a reward for good behavior.

Interestingly, goblins have their own folklore regarding the power of stinkworms. For example, it's said that if a goblin eats a bowl of fresh stinkworm ears, the eater will absorb the worm's memories of its final days. Given that stinkworms are usually farmed on fresh troll dung, we might question why a goblin would want to have any knowledge of the worm's life. However, valuing another sentient creature's consciousness enough to want to absorb it is just one of many ways that goblins continue to surprise us.

BRIGHT GOBLINS, BIG CITY

Much has been written on the intelligence of goblins. Thanks to my experience working closely with goblins of all ages and status, I can state with confidence that they are a lot brighter than they are so often given credit for. Not only are they capable of navigating the complex social and cultural networks that we have already outlined, but they have an extraordinary talent for inventing and committing new crimes. Within hours of a new Haven City law being passed, goblins across the city will be working out a way around it. Or through it. Or under it. Now, some may say this is using their ingenuity for horrible purposes and is why Howler's Peak is so full at the moment. But another way of looking at it would be to wonder, why doesn't Haven City society use this inventiveness and put it to a more productive use?[15]

Working in the Goblin Correctional Facility has given me a unique perspective on goblins, their lives, and their society. They are fascinating creatures who deserve our respect and an invitation to participate more in Haven City society.

[15] Editor's Note: General warning—just don't let them ever guard chickens. It never ends well.

GOBLIN LIFE TOO HECTIC?
NO TIME TO EVEN LICK YOUR OWN EYEBALLS?
WE CAN DO IT FOR YOU. PROFESSIONAL
EYEBALL LICKERS AVAILABLE NOW.

CALL FOR RATES.
HAVEN CITY

HUNGRY?

GOBLIN MASTER CHEF PREPARES STIR-FRIED ORGANIC STINK-WORM EARS AND DELIVERS TO YOU WITHIN THE HOUR.

CALL HAVEN CITY

NO TIME WASTERS OR WE'LL SET GENERAL SCALENE ON YOU.
HAVE YOU RECENTLY BEEN THE VICTIM OF A CRIME? HA-HA. IT WAS PROBABLY US. BETTER KEEP YOUR MOUTH SHUT. WE KNOW WHERE YOU LIVE (PROBABLY).

UNATTACHED LONELY GOBLIN SEEKS SIMILAR FOR MIDNIGHT WALKS, ROMANTIC TALKS, AND STINKWORM SUPPERS. SEND RECENT HOLOGRAPH TO P.O. BOX 616 HAVEN CITY.

CHAPTER 6

GNOMES

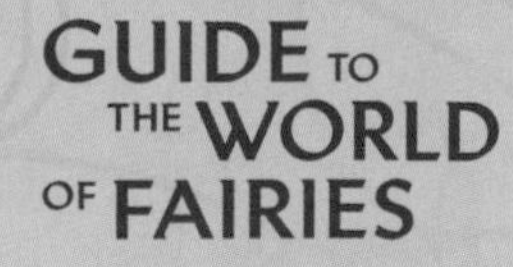

GNOMES ARE ONE OF THE OLDEST AND MOST RESPECTED OF THE FAIRY RACES. GNOMES LOVE GOLD AND GEMS NEARLY AS MUCH AS US DWARFS. OKAY, MAYBE JUST AS MUCH AS DWARFS. SOMETIMES SAID TO BE THE ORIGINATORS OF FAIRY MAGIC THANKS TO THEIR DEEP CONNECTIONS TO THE EARTH, GNOMES ARE QUIET, DETERMINED CRAFTSPEOPLE WHO GET THE JOB DONE. THIS CHAPTER CONTAINS EVERYTHING YOU EVER WANTED TO G-KNOW ABOUT GNOMES. (GET IT?! I'M SPOILING YOU.)

OUR FEATURE ARTICLE IS BY T. J. FLEETSTREAM, AN ELF WHO IS EMPLOYED BY THE HAVEN CITY FAIRY COUNCIL AS AN INCLUSIVITY AND DIVERSITY OFFICER, WHICH ACTUALLY MEANS IT'S HER JOB TO GET GNOMES TO JOIN IN WITH MORE THINGS AND TAKE PART IN SOCIAL STUFF. ANYWAY, WE START WITH OUR SPOTTER'S GUIDE.

SPECIES: Gnome

LOOKS LIKE: One of the smallest of the fairy races, standing at about two feet tall. Most gnomes are both portly and stocky.[1]

SIZE: About two feet tall, with big personalities.

PERSONALITY: Determined.

MOST LIKELY TO BE CAUGHT DOING: Their job.

MOST EASILY SPOTTED WHEN: Asleep on a pile of gold coins snoring like a pig in a poke.

[1] Editor's Note: Sorry, gnomes, you know it's true.

Encrypted Message

Hello, Butler.

There are so many opportunities for us to exploit the world of our fairy friends that it's hard to know where to start, even if you are a genius with an IQ higher than a dozen chess computers. I've been collating our data on gnomes today and hope to share it post-dinner. Their love of gold and jewels strikes me as something we can use to our advantage in the future, if you take my meaning. Although perhaps I should also add that they seem a fairly upright race, and although they love gold and treasure, they seem to prefer to actually earn it than steal it. I know, there are some things that even a genius can't understand.

AF II

Listen, I got nothing against gnomes. I've known a lotta great gnomes in my time. They're solid guys. Solid with the magic. Solid with obeying the law. Solid with working hard. These guys are the very definition of solid and reliable.

Sure, they like gold (who doesn't!), but do they ever spend any of it on, say, a wild all-night party and invite their dwarf friends along? Do they ever take a chance and partake in a little grand theft? No. No, they do not. I mean, I guess if you were a Boss type and wanted someone reliable who shows up for work on time every day, takes his responsibilities seriously, works hard, obeys all the rules, and would never let you down, then sure, you could hire a gnome. But I ask you, who wants that?

Mulch

T. J. FLEETSTREAM IS ONE OF HAVEN CITY'S INCLUSIVITY & DIVERSITY OFFICERS. SHE WORKS DIRECTLY FOR THE HAVEN CITY FAIRY COUNCIL TO ENSURE THAT ALL THE FAIRY PEOPLE ARE FAIRLY REPRESENTED IN HAVEN CITY SOCIETY AND ITS INSTITUTIONS.

THERE'S GNOME DOUBT ABOUT IT

By T. J. FLEETSTREAM

I am delighted to have the opportunity to write this article about our gnome population for *What's On in Haven City Magazine*. My role on the council is to ensure that all fairy species are properly engaged and involved in Haven City society. We want all fairies to feel at home in Haven City and like they have a voice. Gnomes are a case in point. If left to their own devices, these quiet, hard-working, and shy fairies have a tendency to keep to themselves. Of course, there are a few gnomes who have immersed themselves in mainstream society; one thinks immediately of the top psychologist Dr. J. Argon, for example. But the majority of gnomes often live solitary lives on the edges of their communities, and it's my job to involve them in more community social activities.

THERE'S NO PLACE LIKE GNOME

Do not be fooled by a gnomes, modest or shy demeanor. As a race, gnomes are very powerful and have a natural affinity for magic. Gnomes tend to keep their magical abilities to themselves, regarding any act of magic as something private.

The name "gnome" means "earth dweller," and it's widely believed in gnome circles that it was the gnomes' closeness to the earth, both physical and spiritual, that led to the Fairy People becoming users of magic tens of thousands of years ago. There's no proof of this, of course, but gnomes are terribly proud of this belief anyway.

The Booke of the People records how many of the most powerful warlocks

WARLOCKS

Warlocks have existed among the Fairy People for as long as anyone can remember. A warlock is a member of a fairy race that has been trained in the use of magic and spells and is now both skilled and powerful.[2]

It is said that the ancient warlocks could use their magic to do almost anything, including turning lead into gold, which possibly explains the huge gold reserves now in the possession of the Fairy Council. Many ancient warlocks, it has been discovered, were gnomes, so their love of gold lends credence to the rumors.

The Council of Warlocks oversees magical matters for the entire Fairy People. The council is made up of thirteen members—one representative from each of the fairy races, along with other powerful and respected warlocks. In recent times the council has tended to stay out of the limelight and avoid the day-to-day politics of Haven City.

Warlocks serve the city in other ways, too. There are paramedic warlocks who use their knowledge of healing magic to attend to injured citizens, particularly L.E.P. officers hurt in the line of duty. Some warlocks can be hired for individual magic spells or assignments such as the recovery of a missing pet.

[2] Editor's Note: Apart from demons, who sometimes become demon warlocks when they hit puberty. See the demon chapter for the juice on that one, warlock fans.

A MEMBER OF HOUSE GOLDBOW, THIS GNOME'S FRIENDLY (ISH) EXPRESSION IS TYPICAL OF THE LAID-BACK INDIVIDUALS WHO CALL THIS HOUSE THEIR HOME.

from the ancient times were gnomes. Not all of them have been good. It is hard, when in control of that much power, to always stay on the side of right. Especially when tempted by gold.

LET GNOME ONE FORGET

One famous gnome (that most would rather forget) is Shayden Fruid. This bad boy betrayed the Fairy People after the Battle of Taillte. He was once known as Shayden the Bold, until he turned traitor to his kind and got himself rebranded as Shayden the Shame of Taillte. Shayden has had more rude songs written about him in the last ten thousand years than any other gnome, and that's saying a lot.

MOBILE GNOMES

Traditionally, gnome society was structured by a rigid house system. The houses were supposed to act like extended family trees, providing support and a unique identity depending on which house a gnome pledged loyalty to. But of late, this system has grown lax, and gnomes now often move between houses if they find a different one appeals more.

The house system does, in theory, give gnomes a sense of belonging, and every half century or so, a house will get together (behind closed doors, of course) for a riotous session of quiet celebration and gnome backslapping.

The main houses in gnome society are as follows:

HOUSE GOLDBOW

One of the oldest houses, centered on earth magic and energy manipulation. An easygoing, welcoming house that stresses a gnome's closeness to nature and their relationship to the earth. If a gnome has no personal affiliations or if their family tree is unknown, they will often petition to be accepted into this house.

HOUSE REDSTONE

A favorite with gnomes who prefer jewels to precious metals. Redstone gnomes are famed for their poetry and prose, usually singing the praises of whatever gemstone they are fascinated by at the time of their performing. This is a peaceful house, its calm interrupted only by the occasional argument about who really wrote the verse about the oak tree in the moonlight or why does nothing rhyme with "orange."

HOUSE GOBB

Members of this house believe they are directly descended from King Gobb, the first king of the gnomes. Gnomes from House Gobb tend to have a slightly superior attitude, and rarely "cross the floor," as changing to another house is called. House Gobb gnomes make the worst dinner-party guests. Once a century or so there are rumors that House Gobb is planning to reassert the gnomes' royal system, but these stories have never come to anything.

HOUSE MOONSTONE

Easygoing, relaxed gnomes identified by their preference for food over gemstones. House Moonstone gnomes tend to be outgoing and gregarious and therefore are more connected to mainstream fairy society than those who belong to other houses.

HOUSE GLINT

This is the most secretive—and perhaps troublesome—of the gnome houses. Members of House Glint worship the increasingly rare black-eyed goblin, and are said to use the creatures in their dark magical rituals. House Glint gnomes have very little interaction with outsiders but have been known to trade magical favors for something that they really want. You cross a member of House Glint at your peril. I usually leave them to their own devices because I find them a bit creepy, to be honest.[3]

GNOME ALONE

Everybody knows that gnomes love gold, silver, and jewels to the point of distraction. They seem to crave the physical presence of the valuable items more than the wealth that they represent. I've known gnomes who would work a grueling day job as a tunnel cleaner rather than cash in any of their gold, even when selling a little could make their life much, much easier. Gnomes live for collecting and hoarding their precious metals and gemstones.

Gnomes are one of the longest-lived of the fairy races, and gnomes over a thousand years old can have very slow metabolisms indeed. An elderly gnome on a pile of gold can easily slip into a state

[3] Editor's Note: You and me both. We've all heard the rumors about Hamburg.

that resembles a deep hibernation and sleep for decades at a time. They seem none the worse for wear when this happens, but the more fairy society changes without them, the less they feel part of it and the more likely they are to hibernate again. One of my jobs is to engage with the elderly gnome community and encourage them to become involved with the modern fairy world again.

GNOME IS WHERE THE HEART IS

Readers of this article might perhaps know a gnome that they haven't seen

AN ELDERLY GNOME DOING WHAT THEY LOVE TO DO BEST—RELAXING WITH THEIR GOLD. ACTUALLY, THEY JUST LOVE THE GOLD. IT DOESN'T MATTER MUCH IF THEY ARE RELAXING.

around in a while. Why not knock and see if your neighbor is all right? There are many simple ways that we can all help senior gnomes avoid social isolation:

1. Arrange a gnome dinner party. Dining out in a social setting can greatly enrich the lives of the elderly.

2. Give them a pet. Studies by elven scientists have shown that having to look after a pet adds decades to the life span of a gnome. Animal companionship increases the quality of life for many gnomes. A simple stinkworm in a box can be enough.

3. Give affection. This year we are launching SUBTERRANEAN GIVE A GNOME A HUG WEEK, in which Haven City citizens will be invited to hug a gnome. It's true that the idea initially had something of a mixed reception in gnome circles.

Any and all of these ideas could make a real difference to an elderly gnome facing social isolation near you.

GNOME SWEET GNOME

Gnomes have taken on some of the toughest jobs in Haven City over the last century. Fire gnomes have saved countless lives with their focused professionalism in emergency situations. The long-serving chief training instructor at the L.E.P. Academy, Paye Tention, is a gnome.

This tradition of quiet, humble public service dates back to the most ancient of times. Gnomes have always been talented craftsmen, and, with their combination of craft and magic, were responsible for helping create many fairy stone monuments.

STANDING GNOMES

Gnomes have always had a deep connection to language, and their native tongue, Gnommish, has become the language of all the People. As a result of this love of language, gnome craftsmen would engrave magical symbols in the rocks of new fairy monuments. The act of adding symbols onto the rocks and therefore onto the landscape of the earth itself was an extremely meaningful one for gnomes. The act charged the sacred sites with energy and connected them to the grid of power points that still spans the entire surface world today.

WHILE RARELY SEEN DUE TO THE SECRETIVE NATURE OF THE GNOMES WHO TAKE PART, THIS IMAGE DEPICTS CRAFTSMEN CARVING THEIR ANCIENT LANGUAGE INTO STANDING STONES, IMBUING THEM WITH MAGIC.

GNOMMISH

Gnommish is the language of the Fairy People. When written down, it appears as a series of symbols resembling eyes, insects, and other combinations of natural elements. It is believed that, as its name suggests, Gnommish originated with gnomes before becoming the most widely spoken and popular of the fairy languages. There are several dialects and different variations of the language in common use today. Gnommish was traditionally written starting at the center of a page and spiraling out to the edges. After a few hundred years, everyone agreed that this gave them blinding headaches. To solve the problem, the now-common horizontal-lines format was adopted, to the relief of absolutely everyone, apart from a family of pixies who made a living selling headache cures.

A B C D E F G

H I J K L M N

O P Q R S T U

V W X Y Z

0 1 2 3 4 5 6 7 8 9

SUMMARY

Through my work, I have seen over the years that gnomes are magical creatures in more ways than one. It is rare that a gnome will push themselves forward as some other fairy races do, but they contribute just as much to our society.[4] There are many things that we can do to include these wise and ancient people more in our lives and we would be all the better to do so. I hope that in giving readers a closer look at this usually reclusive and shy bunch, I will have opened fairies' eyes to how much gnomes have to offer. After all, we wouldn't be able to speak to each other without them. That seems like enough of a reason to give them a chance. Right?

[4] Editor's Note: Pixies—she's looking at you.

CHAPTER 7

GREMLINS

SO IT TURNS OUT THAT IT'S NOT JUST DWARFS THAT ARE UNDERAPPRECIATED BY FAIRY SOCIETY. GREMLINS ARE AS WELL. NOT ONLY ARE THE LITTLE FELLERS SOMETIMES LEFT OFF LISTS OF THE PEOPLE COMPLETELY, BUT THEIR GREAT TALENTS ARE ALSO COMPLETELY OVERLOOKED. OF ALL THE FAIRY RACES, GREMLINS HAVE THE LEAST VISIBLE, BUT MOST EXCEPTIONAL SKILL. GREMLINS ARE SENSITIVE TO THE ENERGY FIELDS OF OBJECTS, AND THEY CAN TELL WHEN SOMETHING IS WRONG. IF IT'S A MECHANICAL THING, THEN THE CHANCES ARE THEY'LL HAVE IT FIXED BEFORE YOU CAN SAY "WHY ARE YOU TAKING MY STUFF APART?!" THE DO-GOODER WHO WROTE ABOUT GNOMES IS ALSO AN EXPERT ON GREMLINS, SO OUR FEATURE ARTICLE COMES TO YOU STRAIGHT FROM THE KEYBOARD OF T. J. FLEETSTREAM AGAIN.[1] WE START WITH OUR SPOTTER'S GUIDE.

SPOTTER'S GUIDE — GREMLINS

SPECIES: Gremlin

LOOKS LIKE: Greenish humanoid with yellow eyes full of expression. They have tiny pointed ears, with small noses and a wide mouth.

SIZE: Gremlins are the smallest of the Fairy People, with adults standing about two feet high.

PERSONALITY: Shy, but always willing to lend a hand.

MOST LIKELY TO BE CAUGHT DOING: Something to help.

MOST EASILY SPOTTED WHEN: Things go wrong and they are accidentally seen.

[1] Editor's Note: No letters were harmed in the making of this sentence.

Encrypted Message

Butler:

Today, I've been trawling the ancient fairy texts for information about gremlins. I was as surprised as you (well, a bit less surprised actually, given my superintelligence) to learn that gremlins are real.

They seem to be the odd-job men of the fairy world, able to see what's wrong with anything and to put it right. Is this amazing skill of theirs something we can use? Not to get something working, but perhaps to do the reverse? Imagine if we could introduce a gremlin into a bank's high-security system and cause the entire system to malfunction and break down at our command.

Now *that* would be interesting. Why don't we discuss it over the weekend? I am far too busy for the next several days with my science fair project preparation. Why my school insists on even having a competition continues to irk me. I win. Every time. I suppose, though, it is good for others to see what they could do—if they had my intellectual capabilities. Ha. See what I did there, Butler? I made a joke. Because really, no one could ever be that smart.

I'll send you a day and time to discuss gremlins further. Till then, please don't be bothered by any loud, booming noises coming from the lab.

AF II

Gremlins and I go way back. Have you ever heard the story about the gremlin and the Bank of Tara? No? Okay, I'll tell you, but you gotta change the name of the bank and my name and probably your name, too. So, here goes, I was planning one last foolproof bank raid on the Bank of Tara jewel vaults. They have maximum security—everyone knows a stinkworm couldn't creep in there undetected. You've got no chance, but you know, I'm Mulch Diggums. I'm not called the Viceroy of Vaults for nothing. In fact I usually have to pay ten bucks to get called that. That's a joke, by the way.

Anyhow, I put together the greatest bank vault team ever assembled. At least the greatest ever assembled on a wet Tuesday afternoon in the Wexford area. This was just after the whole Lady Fei Fei's Tiara thing had gone south. I get a gremlin on the team. Spoonbend Slowly was his name, if I remember rightly. So things start well, he's sensing the bank and the vaults and the security. "This camera here is going to fail in an hour. This laser trap doesn't reach the far side of the corridor, so step there." So it's all going well and I'm thinking this is great, having a gremlin along is the future of bank jobs. We get into the vault and begin redistributing the wealth to some of Haven City's poorest, most deserving, and extremely handsome citizens.[2] Spoonbend won't shut up. He keeps talking. He keeps telling the rest of the team what's going to go wrong. This swag bag is going to break in three hours. Sharkbait Sharky's artificial leg is going to become trapped in one position in three and a half days' time. He started telling one of the guys that he was gonna get a toothache around the time of the next full moon. If you have ever seen a set of dwarf toothy pegs up close then you'll realize that is serious news. So a whole argument-type situation breaks out in the vault, then an actual fight breaks out in the vault. Then I heard the sound of the L.E.P. arriving, so I quickly break out of the vault. I only escaped by the skin of my considerably sized teeth.

Gremlins—you gotta love 'em, but never do a bank job with 'em, cos they won't shut up!

Mulch

[2] Editor's Note: He means himself. You know that, right?

T. J. FLEETSTREAM IS AN ELF AND AN INCLUSIVITY AND DIVERSITY OFFICER FOR THE HAVEN CITY FAIRY COUNCIL. IF YOU READ THE LAST CHAPTER THEN YOU'LL THINK I'M AN IDIOT FOR TELLING YOU AGAIN. BUT APPARENTLY SOME PEOPLE MIGHT READ THIS GUIDE OUT OF ORDER AND NOT HAVE READ THE CHAPTER BEFORE. WHO WOULD READ A BOOK OUT OF ORDER? ANYWAY, OVER TO T. J. FLEETSTREAM.

EVERY LITTLE THING SHE DOES IS MAGIC

By T. J. FLEETSTREAM

GREMLINS IN THE WORKS

In my near century working for the Haven City Fairy Council, I can honestly say I have never met a gremlin that I didn't like. Gremlins are often ignored and nearly always underappreciated.

As a race, gremlins have an extraordinary natural ability to detect energy imbalances in any system. In simpler terms, they can sense when something is not working, identify what is wrong, and more often than not put it right. Whenever—and wherever—things are repaired or invented, you'll likely find a gremlin as a member of the team. They may not be heading up the team, or have any formal qualifications, but when they speak, they'll be listened to.

The gremlins find it very difficult to put into words exactly how they feel when sensing these magical energy

IS IT ME, OR IS THERE SOMETHING ABOUT A GREMLIN'S BIG EYES THAT MAKE THEM COME ACROSS AS MISCHIEVOUS? GREMLINS LOVE TO TRAVEL, EVEN MORE THAN DWARFS DO, AND OFTEN MOVE AROUND UNNOTICED IN THE WORLD OF MUD PEOPLE.

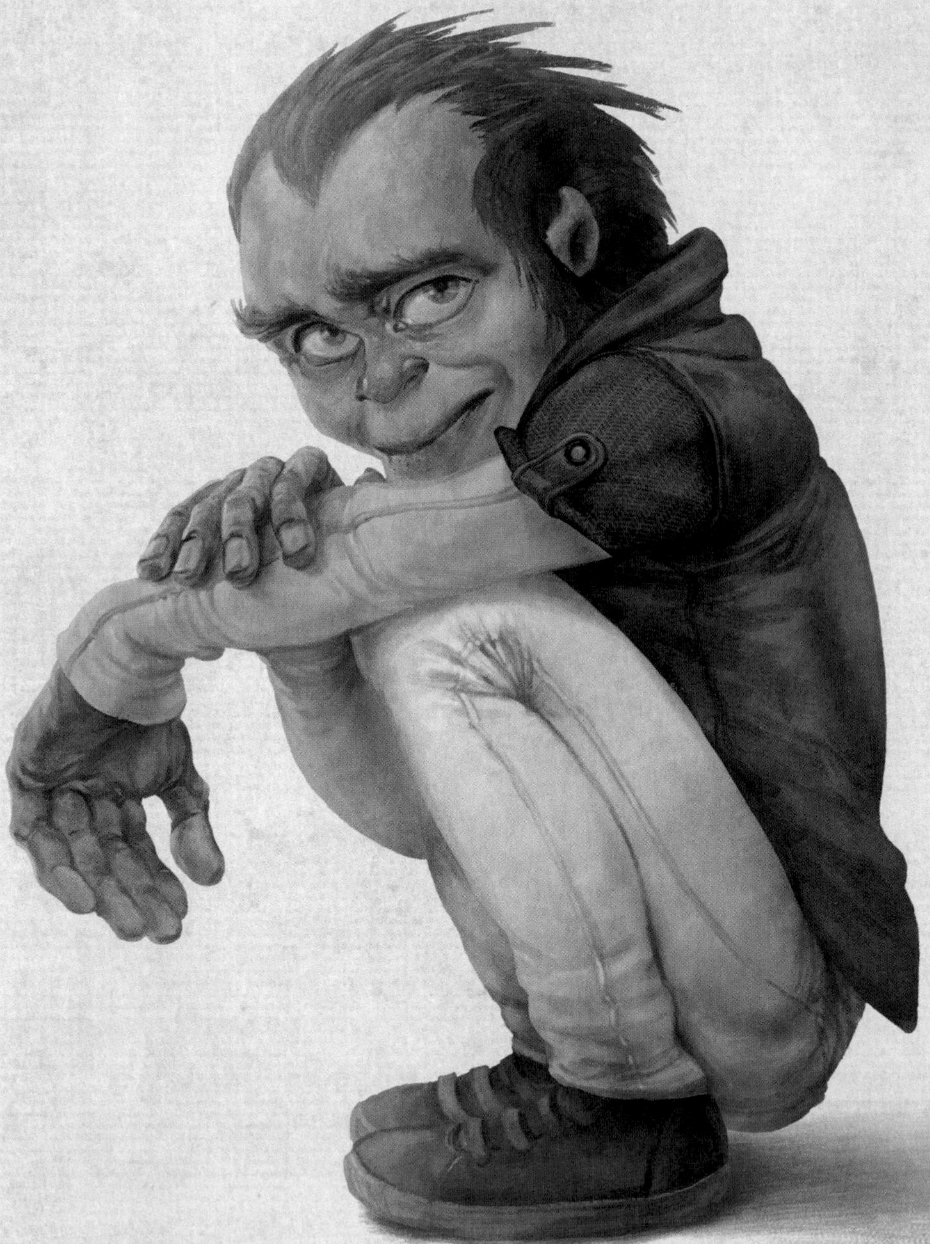

fields. The best explanation I've heard is that it feels like a very strong intuition that they just can't ignore. They have to look, they have to find out what's wrong, and if they can, they have to put it right.

Their ability doesn't just work on mechanical equipment; it applies to living creatures as well. Gremlins have been at the forefront of emergency medical care in Haven City for centuries. If you ever see the emergency services at an accident scene, you'll probably spot a gremlin medic making an examination of the injured.

WHAT'S IN A NAME?

It's a great disappointment to gremlins that they don't enjoy a better reputation. In the distant past, gremlins were feared and regarded as having supernatural powers.[3] It's easy to see how simple Fairy Folk in ancient times could mistake a prediction of something going wrong for a curse being placed.

Gremlins have a particularly bad reputation on the surface world with Mud Men. The entire race of aggressive, polluting, overbreeding Mud People regards gremlins as terrible creatures who deliberately cause machines to break and consequently cause accidents. This strange misconception seems to date from the last time that the Mud People had what they call a "World War."[4]

Drawn to help in the conflict on the surface, gremlins would hide themselves on board aircraft and fly with fighter planes in danger of suffering a mechanical malfunction. Most of the time, the gremlin was able, in complete secrecy, to repair whatever was about to go wrong and prevent any accident. However, on the rare occasion that the damage was too severe to be repaired, there were instances where the gremlin became so panicked that they were seen by the Mud Man fighter pilot in the chaos of the flight. Since gremlins were therefore only seen when aircraft developed a mechanical malfunction, they quickly came to be blamed for accidents, crashes, and general

[3] Editor's Note: Ironic, huh? Fairies frightened of the supernatural.

[4] Editor's Note: A "World War" is a very aggressive competition or disagreement between Mud Men. Fairy People will remember it as "the second time the ground shook in only a few decades; what in Frond's name are they doing up there?"

disasters. That they were labeled evil saboteurs is a great sorrow to the entire gremlin race.

HAVE GREMLIN, WILL TRAVEL

Gremlins love to travel. Even a gremlin with a family will move homes at regular intervals, but a solo gremlin will often spend decades simply traveling around. Gremlins are drawn to help people of all species (fairy and Mud People), and will wander over- and underground doing just that whenever the chance arises. As well as their natural magical ability to spot what's wrong with things, gremlins seem to possess the gift of going unnoticed when they want to. This seems to apply to going mostly unnoticed by Mud Men and also the L.E.P. charged with keeping Fairy Folk underground. Only when a repair attempt goes wrong, as explained in the aircraft example above, do they occasionally and accidentally draw attention to themselves.

WHAT CAN I DO TO HELP?

If gnomes tend to look old before their time, gremlins are the opposite and often have a youthful look that hides their true age. All the fairy races age at different rates. Gnomes, for example, often seem to pass from a youthful teenage appearance straight into early old age, where they stay for centuries.

Chronic loneliness among the elderly gremlin population is a serious issue, and it's getting worse. If you live next door to an elderly gremlin, please be a good neighbor and check up on them a few times a decade. Likewise, if you notice a new younger gremlin face in your area, why not make the first move by saying hello and inviting them over for a pot of stinkworm tea? A little effort can make a lot of difference.

Looking forward, I'd like to see more gremlins take their rightful place in Haven City society, and for them to stop being the forgotten fairy race. With care and work, I think that can happen.

CHAPTER 8

DWARFS

WHAT CAN I SAY ABOUT DWARFS THAT HASN'T BEEN SAID ALREADY? PLENTY, FOR THOSE SO-CALLED REPORTERS OFTEN FOCUS ON THE NEGATIVE WHEN, REALLY, THEY SHOULD HAVE INFINITELY MORE RESPECT FOR THIS SPECTACULAR SPECIES. OF ALL THE RACES OF THE FAIRY FAMILY, DWARFS ARE THE MOST INTELLIGENT, THE MOST HANDSOME, THE MOST MODEST, AND ALSO, OF COURSE, THE VERY BEST AT WRITING. WHEN IT CAME TO WHO SHOULD BE TASKED WITH WRITING THIS EXTREMELY IMPORTANT CHAPTER ON THE MOST IMPORTANT FAIRY SPECIES AND HELP SHED LIGHT ON HOW GREAT THEY ARE, THERE WAS A SHORTLIST OF ONE. I WAS DUTY BOUND TO CHOOSE THE SMARTEST, MOST KNOWLEDGEABLE DWARF THAT I KNOW, AND SO, WITH ALL DUE HUMILITY, I'D LIKE TO SAY HOW HAPPY I WAS TO TAKE THE JOB OF DESCRIBING DWARFS AND THEIR WORLD TO OUR MANY (HOPEFULLY!) READERS. WE START, AS ALWAYS, WITH OUR SPOTTER'S GUIDE AS TO WHAT MAKES A DWARF A DWARF.

SPOTTER'S GUIDE — DWARFS

SPECIES: Dwarf.

LOOKS LIKE: A dwarf in his prime is without doubt one of the finest sights in all creation, and I'm not even exaggerating a tiny bit.

SIZE: Most dwarfs are about three feet tall. (For some dwarfs, that's their waist measurement, too.)

PERSONALITY: Dwarfs tend to be kind, considerate, and not at all greedy about gold. They have zero propensity for thieving, stealing, nicking stuff, or other nefarious deeds.

MOST LIKELY TO BE CAUGHT DOING: Something that looks like a crime but isn't.

MOST EASILY SPOTTED WHEN: They have just unleashed a trouserful of dwarf gas, although you may not be conscious long enough to notice it.

Encrypted Message

Butler,

Dwarfs will do anything to get their hands on gold and they will stop at nothing for a pocketful of jewels. They have a wide variety of amazing abilities and very few morals.

They are, by far, my favorite fairy race.

These are definitely people that we can do—and, of course, already have done—business with, and my infinite-sized mind is already full of brilliant ideas for future endeavors. (Before you point it out, Butler, yes, if my mind were literally infinitely large, then it could never be full up, but it's a sign of how excited I am about teaming up with a certain dwarf again that I'm prepared to overlook my own inexact turn of phrase.) When you are back from shooting practice, please head upstairs.

AF II

HEY, NORD! I'M STILL WAITING FOR A STRAIGHT ANSWER. DO YOU WANT ME TO WRITE THE CHAPTER ON DWARFS OR . . . NOT? I'M WORKING OVER THE WEEKEND ON A JOB THAT REQUIRES STEALTH AND SILENCE, SO PLEASE DON'T RING ME IN CASE THE SECURITY GUARDS HEAR MY PHONE.

MULCH

NORD DIGGUMS WAS BORN AT AN EARLY AGE. IN FACT, ZERO. AND THEN I, OOPS, I MEAN HE, STARTED GETTING OLDER EVERY DAY AFTER THAT. IT'S OFTEN BEEN REMARKED (USUALLY BY ME) THAT NORD IS SO GOOD-LOOKING, HE IS EVEN HANDSOME IN COMPLETE DARKNESS. NORD HAS DONE THINGS AND DONE TIME. HE WAS AWARDED TREMBLING BEARD OF THE YEAR BY HIS TUNNEL FAMILY FOR THREE DECADES RUNNING, AND NOT ONLY THAT BUT CONSECUTIVELY, TOO. HIS BEST-SELLING, AWARD-WINNING AUTOBIOGRAPHY *'TUNNEL VISION* IS BOUND TO BE COMMISSIONED SOON. YOU MAY RECOGNIZE NORD FROM HIS TIME AS PRODUCT AMBASSADOR FOR DIGGER'S DELIGHT—THE FRESH MOUTH SPRAY DESIGNED TO MAKE YOUR MOUTH AS FRESH AS IT WAS JUST BEFORE YOU STARTED EATING THROUGH RAW EARTH. LAWSUITS RESULTING FROM USE OF THIS PRODUCT SHOULD BE REFERRED DIRECTLY TO THE MANUFACTURES AND NOT ME. I MEAN NOT NORD. NORD DIGGUMS IS THE MORE HANDSOME, MORE FAMOUS COUSIN OF THE LESS HANDSOME, LESS FAMOUS MULCH DIGGUMS.[1]

LIGHT AT THE END OF THE TUNNEL, OR MY LIFE AS A DWARF

By NORD DIGGUMS

Famed for their handsome sophistication, dwarfs are born to tunnel. In the same way that sprites fly, trolls eat, and krakens . . . well, krakens don't do anything at all . . . dwarfs are all about the tunneling. As such, tunneling, the effects of tunneling, and the general biological makeup needed to tunnel are the focus of this fantastical and witty piece of entirely true and well-researched writing. Really, you should be thrilled that you are going to hear about the unique skill set that makes dwarfs so amazing from one of the most amazing dwarfs around. Literature does not get better than this, folks.

[1] Editor's Note: Sorry, Mulch, but you know it's true. Ha, here I am footnoting myself to say that I totally agree with myself and what myself said about myself above.

GOING UNDERGROUND

Fairy evolution has given the modern dwarf the perfect biological equipment for tunneling underneath the surface of the earth with both speed and efficiency. Every dwarf has a winning smile—you know it's true, ladies—and here's why. To begin the process of digging, a dwarf unhinges his lower jaw so that he is able to excavate the tunnel with his mouth, chomping through the layers of earth using nothing more than his teeth to make progress. Dwarfs have a very impressive set of toothy pegs, to which anyone who has done amateur dentistry with a dwarf would attest.

DANGEROUS EMISSIONS

To enable dwarfs to chew through the earth at a rate of knots, dwarfs have an accelerated system of digestion that allows the earth to pass through

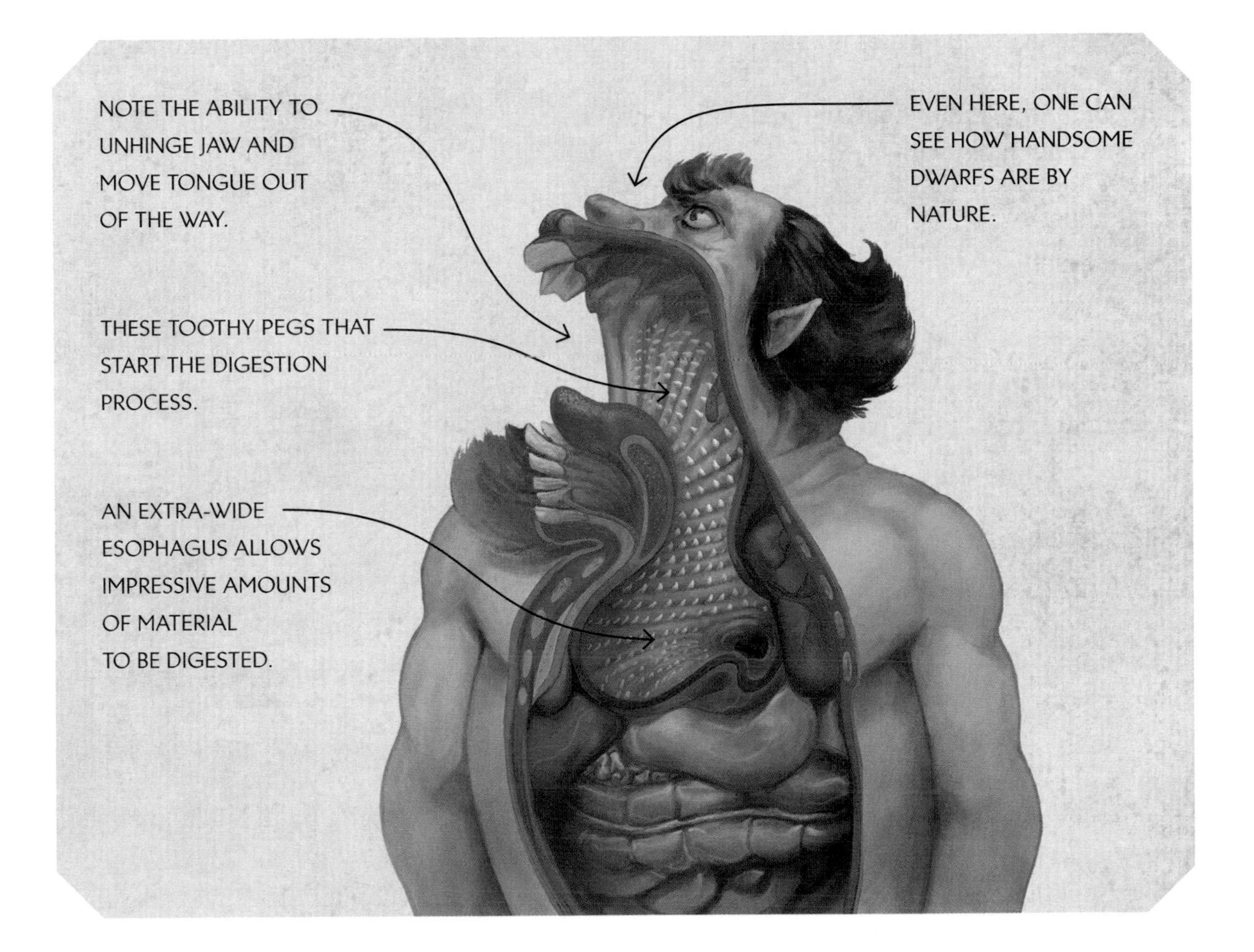

their body and (there's no nice way to say this) out the other end. There's an awful lot of air in most layers of soil. This can quickly build up inside a dwarf with devastating consequences. If the buildup of "dwarf gas" goes unchecked, anything can happen: from minor pains for the poor dwarf, to ultimately a huge catastrophic blowout akin to a small nuclear device going off while hidden in someone's back pocket.

INTERNAL AFFAIRS

A dwarf's body has a kind of emergency detox reflex in case of extreme circumstances like bad diet, trapped dwarf gas, and stress. When a dwarf's heart rate rises over two hundred beats per minute, a dwarf may complete a process known in dwarf circles as "trimming the weight." In such a situation, a dwarf can, in under five seconds, jettison up to a third of his own body weight. This raw material (dwarf gas, loose-layered runny fat, and half-digested food) is often blown out with a great force called a dwarfman's hose. It can be an awe-inspiring sight, or a dreadful one, depending upon where you are standing. Some dwarf yoga instructors claim they can teach a dwarf to trigger this process at will, but for most dwarfs, it's an emergency reflex for when circumstances become too much.

Now let's consider the pores of a dwarf. Intriguing, right? You know you want to hear more.

Well, since you asked . . . Dwarf pores are very talented little things. Not only can they give off moisture in the form of sweat, but they are able to take in moisture, too. This is a very useful survival skill if you owe money and are hiding underground for a while. In all seriousness, dwarf scientists (by which I mean scientists who *study* dwarfs, not scientists who *are* dwarfs) believe that this ability evolved to save the lives of dwarfs trapped by a cave-in during their digging. It means that we are able to drain life-giving moisture from the earth or rocks around us. Both male and female dwarfs can do this with equal and amazing skill.

BUT, and this is a big BUT (well, that's a capital-letters BUT—I don't know if the people publishing this can make the type larger for a properly BIG BUT, but either way, I digress), there are other ways in which a dwarf's pores can be useful. If a dwarf were to make themselves really thirsty by, say, going without water for a day or

AUNT TILDA HAS ALWAYS BEEN ASHAMED BY HER LACK OF BEARD. BUT SHE IS STILL ABLE TO USE HER PORES TO DRAIN WATER FROM EARTH AND ROCKS. I REMEMBER HER ASTOUNDING ME WITH HER WATER DRAINING SKILLS AT MY FIFTH BIRTHDAY PARTY. WHAT A DAY THAT WAS!

so, then their pores open to the size of pinholes and start sucking at anything they touch. Like, for example, the side of a building. Now, you might think, *Why would any law-abiding citizen who wasn't thinking of committing a daringly impossible jewel robbery on the thirteenth floor of a thirteen-floor building want to climb up the side of said building?* and you'd be right. So let's just move along.

Another fantastic adaptation we dwarfs have is one that is super helpful

GETTING BEHIND BOTTOM BURPS

DWARFS HAVE A SPECIAL CLASSIFICATION SYSTEM FOR WHAT WE POLITELY AND BRILLIANTLY CALL OUR BOTTOM BURPS. THIS DESCRIPTIVE SYSTEM IS STRICTLY ADHERED TO BY DWARFS ALL UNDER THE WORLD. DWARFS ARE RIGHTLY PROUD OF THEIR OWN CHEEK SQUEAKS, AND HIGHLY CONTENTIOUS AND UNPLEASANT DEBATES CAN QUICKLY FLARE UP AROUND MISREMEMBERED EXAMPLES OF LETTING POLLY OUT OF JAIL.

THE SCALE OF TROUSER TRUMPETING RUNS AS FOLLOWS:

SHIRT FLAPPER

Similar to standing in a gentle breeze on a warm summer's day. This most gentle of rear-end emissions is the lowest level that our scale of bottom burps takes notice of. This is a light emission that would hardly inflate a small toy balloon. Also known as "Orchestra Practice."

NASAL TICKLER

This causes a noticeable breeze along with other less pleasant side effects. Most dwarfs would be embarrassed to mention this low-level grunt gurgler.

PANTS RIPPER

This is a stronger blast with enough force to cause damage to most fabrics. Among very deep tunnel dwarfs this is known as a "One-Man Salute."

NAUGHT TO SIXTY

An extremely powerful blast that accelerates whoever dropped it to dangerous speeds. Also known as a "Mouse on a Motorcycle" for obvious reasons.[2]

STRAP YOURSELF DOWN

This is the strongest blast you can get without risking rear damage to

[2] Editor's Note: I've never understood that one, and always been too embarrassed to ask. If you understand it, why not write in and let us know?

the emitting dwarf. As the name suggests, a Strap Yourself Down results in the dwarf in question achieving flight for a period of time of no less than five seconds. It is also, due to a dwarf's passion for tunneling, one of the more common of the "trumpets," especially among older members of the species.

DARK SIDE OF THE MOON

Some dwarfs say this is a legend; others claim it's true. A few even claim to have witnessed it themselves. A Dark Side of the Moon is defined as a blast of dwarf gas powerful enough to propel a dwarf into temporary orbit. Rumors have circulated within the dwarf community for years that it was a Dark Side that led to the disappearance of the much-loved dwarf Fisher the Flatulent. Ridiculed by his fellow dwarfs about his lack of exceptional windiness one afternoon, Fisher stormed out of his cave (leaving both a bad atmosphere and bad smell behind him). He was last seen heading up the East Charlton mountain range muttering to himself that he would "show them all!"

He was never seen again, and many people believe he attempted, and succeeded in, producing one final bottom blast so powerful that it propelled the foolish fellow into orbit. Given a dwarf's ability to survive in harsh conditions, it's quite possible that Fisher the Flatulent survived his orbital odyssey and crashed back down to Earth somewhere, and even now is making the long journey home. It's also quite possible that his disappearance was caused by a family argument about who ate the last cat-flavored donut.

NOTE THE ABSOLUTE CONCENTRATION ON THIS HANDSOME DWARF'S FACE. WHILE HIS HEAD OF HAIR IS IMPRESSIVE, IT IS THE USE OF THE SINGLE BEARD HAIR THAT IS TRULY AWE-INSPIRING.

if you were thinking of going into the lock-picking business or thinking of breaking in somewhere, which is obviously something dwarfs would never do. This adaptation is, of course, our beards.

It's not just that dwarfs are great at picking locks, although we are. It's that dwarfs have the perfect lock pick growing right out of their chins. (Yep, I'm talking about both daddy and mommy dwarfs. How's that for equality?) The hairs on a dwarf are not just there to keep us warm.

In fact, they are not really hairs at all, but more like a network of very sensitive antennae that probably evolved to help us dwarfs find our way around underground.[3] Once a dwarf hair is plucked from the dwarf, it quickly stiffens into a form of rigor mortis. However, if pushed into a lock just before rigor mortis occurs, then the hair will assume the shape of the lock's interior.[4] Seconds later, when it hardens, you're holding the perfect lock pick. For the record: Obviously, dwarfs would never take advantage of this fact to enable them to gain entry to banks and jewelers, both places where they have no interest in being anyway. Add to those extraordinary abilities the fact that our saliva hardens on contact with the open air and also glows(!) and I think you'd have to agree that we dwarfs are a rather unusual and amazing species.

UNDERGROUND MOVEMENTS

Dwarfs are social animals and enjoy the company of other dwarfs.[5] There are several ancient and secret organizations that dwarfs can belong to depending on their skills and chosen profession.

Some of the most important of these secret underground brotherhoods of dwarfs are:

THE ANCIENT AND WORSHIPFUL ORDER OF DOOR BREAKERS

One of the oldest dwarf lodges dates back to a time when Mud People had only just invented doors and breaking into them was considered new, cutting-edge technology. This lodge includes many of the great dwarf house burglars of the last thousand years. Members agree to give 5 percent of their yearly "earnings" into lodge funds, although in practice no one ever does.

THE ANCIENT AND WORSHIPFUL ORDER OF TUNNEL SNIFFERS

Once all fairies were forced to relocate underground, dwarfs quickly realized that they had a skill set that could be in high demand. They, unlike any other species, could dig out fresh tunnels—and quickly. There was a rush to hire the best tunnel-digging dwarfs, and a new lodge quickly formed around the expanding underground trade. Members of this order are about as close to

[3] Editor's Note: I'll be honest, I have no idea what I'm talking about here.

[4] Editor's Note: Young dwarfs, remember: Always ask a grown-up permission before you try this at home!

[5] Editor's Note: Or anyone, really, we're not fussy creatures.

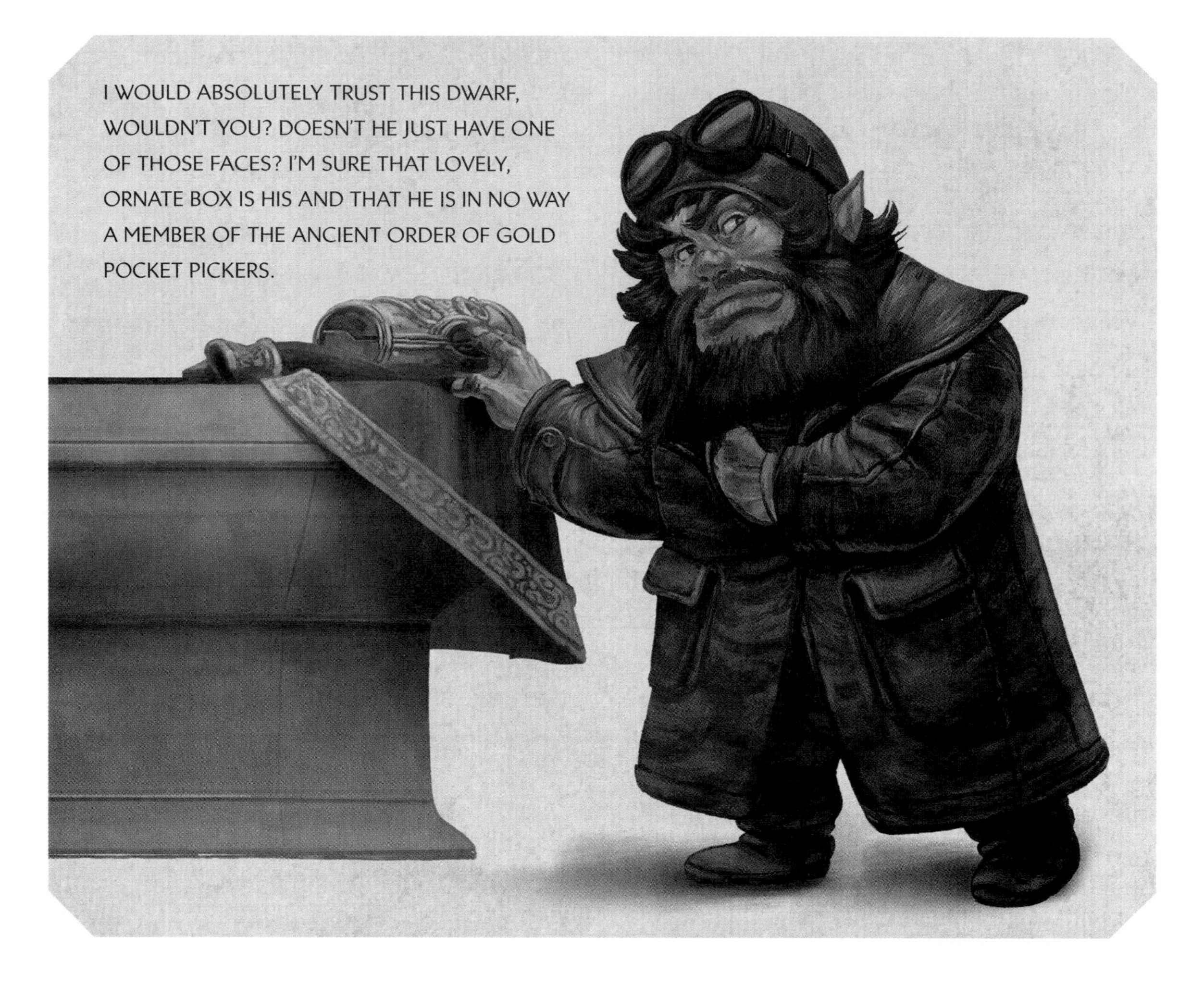

law-abiding dwarfs as you are likely to get (apart from Sparkies).

THE ANCIENT ORDER OF GOLD POCKET PICKERS

For those dwarfs who were worried about losing their magic by breaking the Rule of Dwelling and entering a Mud Person's home without an invitation and so did not want a life of crime (not that what we do is a crime, really—it's a living), another option presented itself. This was the option of earning a living by working the crowds in any jam-packed place and relieving the unwary of the contents of their pockets. Members of this order take great pride in the daily practice of their craft and regard getting spotted as the ultimate shame and humiliation.

THE NOT-SO-ANCIENT BUT STILL-WORSHIPFUL ORDER OF SPARKS[6]

A comparative babe in arms of the ancient dwarf orders, this particular order came into existence because in recent years dwarfs have been flocking to the trade of electrician. Many dwarfs with growing families found they no longer cared for the time away from home that regular jail sentences meant, so they turned to this trade. It makes sense. Dwarfs are natural electricians. They need no lighting to work, are comfortable in the smallest spaces, and are able to dispose of most waste by eating it. Old copper wire is considered a particular treat due to its cleansing properties.

THE ANCIENT AND WORSHIPFUL ORDER OF MUCK MANGLERS AND DOSH DANGLERS

In old dwarf, a "muck mangler" is any dwarf who will move large quantities of earth or rocks from one location to another. The term is most often used for traveling dwarfs who are paid to remove the rubble left after the construction of a new underground dwelling. History tells of many instances of the old "One-Two, Gold in My Shoe" scam, where one dwarf was paid to remove rubble from one property, only to dump it in another property. The owner of that property then hired a second dwarf, who removed the rubble, dumping it back in the original starting location. If well timed and enacted, such a scam has been known to work for several decades and provide a good living for both the dwarfs involved. Unfortunately, this practice has come under the annoying (I mean watchful) eye of the L.E.P., and so it is not as common as it once was, thus depriving many upstanding dwarfs of a decent living.

WRAPPING UP WHAT'S WHAT

In summary, I hope this chapter has proved that dwarfs are among the most friendly, most jovial, best-looking, and well-intentioned of all the Fairy Folk. Make friends with a dwarf and you have a friend for life or until you run out of money, whichever comes first.

POSTSCRIPT: I'm only too aware that the top-quality writing of this chapter will, no doubt, make it easily the reader's favorite out of all the chapters in the book (with the possible exception of the introduction which, of course, I also wrote. There's not much an author such as my immesnsely talented self can do about about that except be nice to the other inferior authors if you write in).

[6] Editor's Note: And believe me, this name was the subject of a lot of debate.

CHAPTER
9

KRAKENS

OF ALL THE FAIRY RACES, THE GREAT AQUATIC KRAKEN IS THE MOST MYSTERIOUS. A HUGE BEAST AFLOAT ON THE GREAT OCEANS OF THE WORLD AND HIDING IN PLAIN SIGHT IN A WORLD OVERRUN BY MUD PEOPLE. IN THIS CHAPTER, CAPTAIN JAC CUZTARD, HEAD OF THE L.E.P.'S KRAKEN WATCH UNIT AND WORLD EXPERT ON THE MIGHTY BEASTS, TELLS US EVERYTHING WE NEED TO KNOW.

AS ALWAYS, WE START WITH OUR SPOTTER'S GUIDE.

SPOTTER'S GUIDE KRAKEN

SPECIES: Kraken.

LOOKS LIKE: A large island or a piece of coastland.

SIZE: Big. Huge. Massive. Really, really large. Honestly, I'm not even joking. Some of them are four miles long!

PERSONALITY: Quiet. Really quiet. Apart from the bit when it explodes. We'll get to that.

MOST LIKELY TO BE CAUGHT DOING: Nothing.

MOST EASILY SPOTTED WHEN: It blasts its entire shell from its back in a high-velocity explosion. *Boom!* This happens only once or twice in the millennia-long life of the kraken.

Encrypted Message

Butler:

I'm amazed, and that doesn't happen often to someone with a genius-level IQ. It's turning out that so many creatures we thought were just myth actually exist. There is a whole multitude of things that have been secreted away from the eyes of Homo sapiens by our fairy friends.

Have you heard of the kraken? It's a legendary sea monster that is said to be the size of an island. There are several reports of early explorers sighting them in the waters of the North Atlantic Ocean. My research has led me to believe that not only are they real, but they are distantly related to the Fairy People. I don't yet know how we can use this knowledge to our financial advantage.

Despite the lack of obvious monetary potential, I think the kraken is definitely worth further research. I'm writing a second neuro-algorithm right now to analyze any unexplained changes in coastlines as recorded on maps from 1500 to 1900, as well as one that highlights areas of unexplained ship disappearances.

Please meet me in my study after your unarmed combat training session (assuming you can still walk), and we'll go through the details.

AF II

I HAVE NEVER MET A KRAKEN, BUT I FEEL THAT WHEN I DO, I WILL IMMEDIATELY COUNT IT AMONG MY CLOSEST FRIENDS. NOW, YOU MAY ASK WHAT IT IS THAT WOULD CREATE SUCH A STRONG EMOTIONAL BOND BETWEEN A HUGE FLOATING-ISLAND-SEA-MONSTER-TYPE THING AND THE WORLD'S MOST HANDSOME DWARF. ONE WORD: METHANE.[1]

IT'S IMPOSSIBLE TO TALK ABOUT KRAKENS AND DWARFS WITHOUT MENTIONING THAT BOTH POSSESS THE MOST AMAZING ABILITY TO PRODUCE VAST QUANTITIES OF STINKY METHANE GAS.

METHANE HAS SEEN ME OUT OF SOME EXTREMELY TRICKY SITUATIONS AND HAS PROPELLED ME TO FREEDOM FROM THE CLUTCHES OF THE L.E.P. SEVERAL TIMES. KRAKENS, HOWEVER, DO NOT USE THEIR METHANE-MAKING METHODS FOR SELF-DEFENSE OR PROPULSION, AS WE TUNNEL DWARFS MIGHT. RATHER, A KRAKEN WILL STORE UP SUCH LARGE AMOUNTS OF METHANE IT WOULD PUT A WINDY DWARF TO SHAME, AND THEN IT WILL IGNITE THE WHOLE LOT . . . BLOWING OFF ITS OLD SHELL!

ALL THIS TALK OF KRAKENS REMINDS ME HOW MUCH I REALLY WANT TO MEET ONE. FOR PROFESSIONAL PURPOSES, OF COURSE. YOU SEE, IT ALSO REMINDS ME OF A BRILLIANT PLAN I ONCE FORMULATED WITH MY COUSIN NORD. (FOR THE RECORD, IT WAS MY PLAN THAT HE HAPPENED TO SAY OUT LOUD FIRST.) HOW'S THIS FOR A PERFECT BANK ROBBERY?

1. FIND A KRAKEN.
2. GET THE KRAKEN TO DISGUISE ITSELF AS PART OF A MUD MAN COASTLINE.
3. ENCOURAGE A BANK TO OPEN A BRANCH "NEAR THE SEA" ON THE NEW STRIP OF "LAND."
4. HAVE THE KRAKEN SWIM OFF WITH THE ENTIRE BANK.
5. ROB THE BANK AT YOUR LEISURE.

ADMITTEDLY, THIS PLAN IS NOT WITHOUT ITS CHALLENGES. NAMELY, FINDING A KRAKEN, PERSUADING THE KRAKEN TO TAKE PART IN THE PLAN, AND GETTING A BANK TO BUILD A BRANCH ON THE NEW STRIP OF LAND (ACTUALLY THE HIDDEN KRAKEN). APART FROM THAT, IT'S ALL SMOOTH SAILING!

MULCH

[1] Editor's Note: Mulch's favorite word. Apart from maybe "food."

CAPTAIN JAC CUZTARD HAS COMMANDED THE L.E.P.'S KRAKEN WATCH UNIT FOR NEARLY THREE DECADES AND RUNS A TIGHT SHIP DEDICATED TO PROTECTING THESE RARE CREATURES. CUZTARD IS A WORLD-RECOGNIZED EXPERT IN UNDERWATER CRIMES AND HAS HAD A LIFELONG INTEREST IN MAGICAL AND SEMI-MAGICAL AQUATIC CREATURES. JAC IS AN ELF WHO FEELS AS AT HOME IN THE DEEP BLUE SEA AS HE DOES ON LAND.

SLIDES UP! KRAKENS REVEALED

By CAPTAIN JAC CUZTARD

IT'S a great honor to be asked to contribute a chapter to this guide to the Fairy People, even if the antics of my mysterious commissioning editor have been a little cloak-and-dagger at times![2]

As a basis for this chapter, I have used my lecture "Kraken Watch 101," which I normally give to new recruits of the L.E.P.'s small, but enthusiastic, Kraken Watch team. This is partly because I feel the lecture deserves a wider, more mainstream audience and partly because the fee being paid is smaller than an undernourished shrimp![3]

I always start my lecture with a slide that says it all in one simple sentence.

Actually, I usually start with a slide that says:

Captain Jac Cuztard, head of L.E.P. Kraken Watch.

[2] Editor's Note to Self: Remember to cut this.

[3] Editor's Note to Self: Outrageous! Must remember to cut this!

It is accompanied by a photo of me receiving the L.E.P. Diver of the Year award (eight wins out of the last ten years!). Then, come to think of it, there are usually a few safety announcements about which emergency exits to use in case of flooding due to an attack by an extremely large underwater predator (the lecture is often given on an L.E.P. submarine), and then (finally!) there is the slide that says it all in one simple sentence:

The kraken is the largest and most magnificent creature that has ever existed in the history of the earth.

Words cannot describe the wonder of the kraken, which is why at this point in the slideshow, I also have a picture of it to show new recruits.[4] Smart, eh? However, the problem with using a graphic is getting a good sense of scale. Any picture showing the whole body of a kraken would reduce a fairy on the same scale to little more than a dot on-screen. And that's why I also include a slide with a photograph of me as a cute bright-as-a-gnome's-button ten-year-old elf holding up a drawing of a kraken to

CAPTAIN CUZARD NOTES: THIS IS THE SLIDE I USE TO GIVE A SENSE OF THE KRAKEN'S SIZE. NOT IMPRESSED YET? THEN LET ME TELL YOU THAT THIS IS TINY TIM, THE SMALLEST OF THE KNOWN KRAKENS.

[4] Editor's Note: Yeah? Well, since I'm paying you, you'd better try, Captain Wavewatch.

show exactly how long ago kraken fever took hold in my tender mind!

Then I have a slide labeled *Legends of the Kraken!* And this is when I talk about what, exactly, a kraken is.

It's not hard to understand why I have always felt such an affinity for these creatures. The kraken is a mighty beast. It is, in fact, the last survivor of a long-passed age of giants. Specimens have been recorded as long as three miles. As far as fairy science knows, they are the largest living things that have ever existed on, or below, our planet.

The earliest records we have of sightings of the mighty kraken are from the unreliable archives of Mud Men. The thirteenth-century saga *Örvar-Oddr* tells of regular sightings of a kraken in the Greenland Sea. The Mud Men named the creature a "lyngbakr," which in their language meant "heather back." The story tells how Mud Men sailing the ocean mistook the huge kraken for an island and moored their ship to it, sending sailors ashore to look for food and fresh water. Of course, when the Mud Morons began to stomp around on the back of the kraken, the poor sensitive creature became frightened and simply sank beneath the waves, accidentally dragging the unfortunate ship and crew into the depths with it. Later, sailing captains feared the kraken, not for any direct danger, but because of the deadly giant whirlpool that was created as it submerged beneath the waves.

Mud Men have never been the most reliable of creatures (as any fairy who has been unfortunate enough to have had dealings with them well knows), and in the seventeenth century, the peaceful island-sized kraken became confused with another creature in the humans' seafaring stories. Mud Men sailors told terrifying stories of how "the kraken" would use its long tentacles to attack ships, crushing their hulls and dragging their screaming crews underwater. These attacks, of course, were not by the kraken but were rather the work of the deadly, terrifying . . .

At this point, I change slides to show a close-up of a very friendly squid.

This always gets a big laugh, and folks have often come up to me after a lecture to say they had expected it to be really dull and serious, but in fact it was great fun, and they didn't know that I could be so funny and interesting. The squid in question is called Sliddberry, and for a while he kinda helped Kraken Watch put some deep-sea monitors in place in the Arctic. He's a great guy and works hard for a bucket of garlic-fried whitebait.

When the laughter finally dies down, I assure the audience that any attacks on Mud Men ships were the work of the occasionally aggressive giant squid, not the docile, slow-moving kraken.

After that, I get into the more modern issues of krakens and their role in the world. Usually I have a slide that says just that. Or sometimes I change it up and it says *Habits of the Kraken*. Depends on my mood, really. Changing stuff around, even a little bit, keeps the talk nice and fresh.

It is easy to appreciate that as Mud Men used their little wooden sailing ships to spread like a virus across the surface of our beautiful planet, krakens were forced to become ever better at hiding. They accomplished this by attaching themselves to coastlines, usually arriving under cover of darkness, and then adopting the brilliant hiding technique of simply staying very still for centuries.

Mud Men are usually so busy polluting and destroying the planet that if they wake up one morning to find that the coastline is a little farther out than it was the night before, they don't care. This new piece of coast is, of course, a kraken that has moved in to nest near a Mud Man port.

Here I show a slide that looks like a normal stretch of coastline, and I surprise the audience by revealing that it's actually a kraken that attached itself to the rocky shore many centuries ago. The irony is that once when I was giving the talk at a water sprite convention, I somehow got all my slides mixed up and ended up showing a photo of a stretch of real coastline! I've kind of kept it in the lecture ever since as a little joke for myself.

It is believed that the world's oldest known kraken, Shelly, took up his position posing as a small island in the Helsinki harbor over five centuries ago. His exact location is known only to a handful of Kraken Watch personnel with the highest security clearance.[5]

[5] Editor's Note: Yeah, yeah.

Once a kraken is settled and has moored itself and committed to a new home, it will usually stay in that location for centuries if conditions remain favorable. Krakens can feed on either food or magical energies. For food, they often position themselves near Mud Man ports, where sadly there is a regular flow of wasted foodstuff into the oceans. Even after the food dries up, a kraken will take a few decades to notice and a few more to decide to do something about it.[6] Changing location seems often to be a course of last resort to these amazing animals.

Food is filtered through a kraken's huge vibrating gills. Unsuitable materials are caught on the gills and ejected, while food matter passes into one of many stomach sacs inside the kraken. Over time, the powerful acids of the kraken's guts break down the food, fermenting some of it into a very rich—and dangerous—form of methane.

This is when I put a slide up with a picture of a big explosion—another winner that usually gets a real gasp from the audience.

Methane is what enables the kraken to jettison its old shell once the body of the kraken has grown and needs a larger shell. The process is as amazing as it is explosive. The kraken stores up methane in a series of strategically placed cells between the old shell on top and the new shell underneath. The pressure of the methane gas helps pry off the old shell. The creature then ignites the methane gas, quite simply blowing the old shell to kingdom come. As shells can be up to miles long, that is a huge amount of heavy material flying around.

Few people have witnessed a kraken shell explosion and lived to tell the tale. One of the only reports comes from the early sixteenth century and tells of a Mud Man sailing ship, the HMS *Finn*, which became lost at sea. Sighting an unexpected island, the sailors landed and began to try to dig for fresh water, as well as make a fire to cook fish. They abandoned the island when it began to shake. While fleeing on their boat, they witnessed a huge blast:

"And lo, the island did explode with the most mighty anger and woe! Parts of it flying into the sky, as if thrown by an unseen giant, and landing all around our most piteous vessel."

[6] Editor's Note: I've had flatmates like this.

Almost certainly, this is a firsthand account of Mud Men accidentally setting off a shell detonation with their own ridiculous stupidity.

At this point in my lecture, I have to comply with L.E.P. Kraken Watch safety guidelines and show a slide that reads:

The L.E.P. Kraken Watch guidelines specifically forbid any L.E.P. personnel to attempt any type of cooking on a kraken. The big bang might have started the universe, but another one from a kraken will end yours.

That usually gets a big laugh. I say "usually." It sometimes gets a really big laugh. Depends on the audience.

Krakens are solitary creatures, spending the vast bulk of their long lives alone. The life span of a kraken is without parallel. We measure their lives not in hundreds of years, not even in thousands of years, but in tens of thousands of years. It took me many applications—and I won't even bore you with the number of hours of grant writing—to get the funding for organic shell dating for all the known krakens, but the money was well spent.

The next slide ALWAYS gets a huge gasp from the audience. (Once, one young elf fainted, but that is very unusual.)

The shell scraping taken from old Shelly showed the creature to be well over ten thousand years old.

One explanation for their long life span is a combination of the very slow metabolism of the kraken and the cold-water environment, which acts to stall the aging process. Another reason krakenologists offer is the huge support network surrounding their soft centers. A large kraken will have over a hundred hearts distributed throughout its massive body, with other internal organs also duplicated in many locations. This means that if one—or even several—fails, the animal is easily able to switch the workload to the remaining functioning organs.

ALL BY THEMSELVES

We believe that there are now only a half dozen or so krakens remaining in the world. This population needs protecting and nurturing. The reason for the fall in kraken numbers during the past ten thousand years is very simple: Mud Men.

Individual krakens have been forced to prioritize survival over breeding, and their numbers have fallen. We also believe that the increasing pollution in the world's oceans has interfered with their breeding cycle. Little is known about how krakens breed, with suggestions ranging from "slowly" to "hardly at all." It would be brilliant to think that in the future, Kraken Watch might be able to oversee some kind of kraken breeding program to help repopulate the oceans.

ON THE WATCH

This usually brings me to the end of my slideshow presentation, and I turn my attention to Kraken Watch, which was the point all along. This is the L.E.P.'s special unit charged with monitoring and protecting the remaining krakens. (I usually have a few slides here showing our very comfortable offices underneath Police Plaza and a few shots of my team of officers in various exotic underwater locations around the globe, but I've been told I can't use them in this article, so you'll just have to imagine that bit.[7] Sorry.)

Unlike other fairy-related beings, a kraken lives its life out there in the Mud Man's world, with only its uncanny resemblance to an island to keep it safe from human eyes. One of our many jobs in Kraken Watch is to make sure that Mud Men remain as blissfully ignorant about krakens as they are now. This means being on twenty-four-hour alert to deal with any sudden kraken movements that occur anywhere in the world.

Another important part of our mission is the monitoring of the health and safety of all known surviving krakens. To help with this, we set up a network of biosensors on each kraken. This sends back live information on the creature's temperature, heartbeat, and brain activity. The sensors also record the animal's location and speed and, if it's in the open ocean, its depth. The readings from the world's krakens are monitored by on-duty officers 24/7.

If you're a young officer in the L.E.P., Kraken Watch can offer you a rewarding career combining global travel with cutting-edge science and the privilege of protecting some of the

[7] Editor's Note: Not at the price you wanted for the photos—no!

most amazing creatures on the planet. Although very different and very distant, the krakens are our brethren as much as all other species of the Fairy People are. Who knows what amazing stories are locked in their huge but so far silent brains? We at Kraken Watch are developing ways to communicate with these mighty beasts of the sea. We hope in the future to be able not only to look after them, but to talk to them and hear what they have to say. Who wouldn't want to be part of that when the time comes?[8]

IF YOU LOVE WATCHING LARGE INANIMATE OBJECTS AND THINK YOU MIGHT BE INTERESTED IN A CAREER IN

KRAKEN WATCH,

CONTACT CAPTAIN JAC CUZTARD,

KRAKEN WATCH, FLOOR -16, JUST OFF THE LONG GRAY WINDOWLESS CORRIDOR, UNDERNEATH POLICE HEADQUARTERS, HAVEN CITY.

[8] Editor's Note: Don't all rush at once.

CHAPTER 10

DEMONS

OKAY, SO LET ME TRY AND EXPLAIN DEMONS. LISTENING? GOOD, HERE WE GO, THEN.

EVERY FAIRY HAS, AT ONE POINT OR ANOTHER, READ THE STORIES ABOUT DEMONS IN *THE BOOKE OF THE PEOPLE*. DEMONS WERE ANOTHER RACE OF THE FAIRY PEOPLE. WHEN MUD MEN TOOK OVER THE SURFACE OF THE PLANET, ALL THE FAIRY PEOPLE DECIDED TO GO DEEP UNDERGROUND TO HIDE. ALL, THAT IS, EXCEPT THE ARROGANT DEMONS, WHO REFUSED TO, AND WHO CAST A SPELL ON THEMSELVES AND VANISHED OVERNIGHT.

NO ONE HAS HEARD OF THEM SINCE, RIGHT?

WELL, AS I WAS GATHERING MATERIAL FOR THIS BOOK, I WAS CONTACTED BY A MYSTERIOUS INDIVIDUAL WHO MADE THE MOST EXTRAORDINARY CLAIMS. HE SAID HE HAD WORKED FOR A SECRET ORGANIZATION CALLED SECTION EIGHT, WHICH WAS A HIDDEN, COVERT PART OF THE L.E.P., AND HE WAS RISKING JAIL, OR WORSE, JUST BY TELLING ME ABOUT THEM.[1] PERHAPS MOST AMAZING OF ALL, HE INSISTED THAT SECTION EIGHT KNEW WHERE THE DEMON RACE WAS AND HAD BEEN MONITORING THEM FOR HUNDREDS OF YEARS.

I WAS READY TO DISMISS ALL THIS AS A PILE OF STINKWORM DROPPINGS UNTIL MY PUBLISHER SUGGESTED THAT IT WAS MY PUBLIC DUTY TO LET YOU READ THE CLAIMS AND DECIDE THEIR TRUTH (OR NOT) FOR YOURSELF.[2]

---

[1] Editor's Note: As if speaking to Nord Diggums would ever be a crime!

[2] Editor's Note: Yeah, and it didn't hurt that they also pointed out how there's nothing like a bit of controversy to sell copies of a book!

FOR THE RECORD, I HAVE NEVER MET THE AUTHOR; THE MANUSCRIPT WAS LEFT IN A TRASH CAN IN GOBLIN TOWN FOR ME TO PICK UP.[3] THOSE OF YOU WHO WILL REFUSE TO BELIEVE WHAT YOU READ IN THE FOLLOWING PAGES MIGHT SAY THAT'S WHERE IT SHOULD HAVE STAYED.

EITHER WAY, WE BEGIN THIS CHAPTER WITH THE SPOTTER'S GUIDE TO DEMONS AND IMPS. (IMPS ARE YOUNG DEMONS, BUT YOU KNEW THAT.)

SPOTTER'S GUIDE — DEMONS

SPECIES: Demons. The eighth member of the Fairy Family.

LOOKS LIKE: Juvenile demons, called imps, are gray, plump, and quite cuddly until they hit puberty. Adult demons have horns, armored skin, and sharp talons. Both imps and demons have magical runic symbols that spiral across their skin.

SIZE: Imps stand about three feet tall. Demons are nearer to five.

PERSONALITY: Sometimes hungry. Sometimes grumpy. Sometimes hungry and grumpy.

MOST LIKELY TO BE CAUGHT DOING: Nothing, as they vanished ten thousand years ago. Supposedly.

MOST EASILY SPOTTED WHEN: We find out where they are.

[3] Editor's Note: Of all the stupid places to pick! I ask you. I only just got out alive.

Encrypted Message

Hello, Butler.

I like to think that I'm pretty good at predicting the future (because I am pretty good at everything), but even my incredible intellect didn't predict I'd one day be sitting in my office writing research notes on demons.

Yes, you read that correctly, Butler, demons. It appears that they are a branch of the Fairy Family tree just like elves and pixies. Well, I say "are," but perhaps I should have said "were," because no one has seen a demon for thousands of years.

The Booke of the People contains some absolutely astounding revelations about the history of the demon race. I won't go into detail now, but I will give you a hint. It involves meteors, a moon rock, and a time spell . . . ? It seems extraordinary, but then, everything else we've learned about the Fairy Folk from that book has proved to be deadly accurate.

I'm digesting the information, old friend, and I'll give you a summary as soon as I am home from school. By the way, if you're picking me up tonight in the Bentley, please note that I have to stay late for a remedial class in Advanced Quantum Mechanics. And before you smirk, Butler, I am not in the class; the school has asked me to teach it.

AF II

Yeah, demons . . . So you wanna know about demons, huh? Before I start explaining all my highly detailed and totally up-to-date demon information, can I just check one tiny itty-bitty thing? I'm getting paid for this, whatever I say, right? That money is already in my poor, sad, empty bank account, just like we agreed, yeah?

Well, in that case, let me say that I don't know a whole lot about demons. Sorry if that stings, but them's the breaks. I've never been friends with a demon, or even done a bank heist with a demon. How could I? There aren't any! (But! If there happens to somehow be a demon reading this who would like to do a daringly dynamic bank heist, then please get in touch with your pal, old Mulchy. If, on the other hand, the L.E.P. and Commander Root are reading this, then make sure old beetroot face knows that's just a gag, okay?)

I know that back in the old days, before the rest of the Fairy People went underground, demons were said to be the strongest and most feared fighters in the fairy army. Legends say they were powerful, and handsome, so they clearly had a lot in common with us modern-day dwarfs.

I remember my grandpappy Burper telling us little Diggumses bedtime stories to get us off to sleep in the burrow. One of our favorites was the story of the gargoyle's touch. Grandpappy would tell us, in a whisper, how demon warlocks had the power to turn anyone into stone with a just a single touch of one of their dainty digits. (That would certainly be handy in a bank job!) There was one story where a great demon warlock called Qwan used his gargoyle's touch at the Battle of Taillte to save a whole squad of dwarfs. They were coming under attack from Mud Men with spears and arrows, and Qwan transformed the whole dwarf squad into stone! When the immediate danger was over, Qwan turned them back to flesh again and off they went to win the battle. I'll never forget Grandpappy Burper Diggums leering over us in the darkness and making that hideous face of his as he pretended to turn to stone. None of us little dwarfs slept for a week after that. Happy days!

Mulch

THE AUTHOR OF THIS EXPOSÉ HAS ASKED TO REMAIN ANONYMOUS FOR PERSONAL REASONS. WE HAVE DECIDED TO RESPECT HIS REASONS. (OR *HER* REASONS, IF HE WAS A WOMAN. WHICH HE MIGHT BE.)

DEMONS! THEY'RE HERE! (BUT I'M NOT!)

By ANONYMOUS

Demons have destroyed my life, but it's not their fault. I've lost my job, my home, and my family not because of demons and their secrets but because I think that people should know the truth. I live on the run now. Never sleeping in the same place more than one night. Paying for everything with untraceable cash. All because of who I was and where I worked.

I'm going to tell you the most dangerous secret I know. Actually, it's the only dangerous secret I know. It's not like I know loads of dangerous secrets. I'm not some paranoid conspiracy theorist. (And, Foaly, if you ever get to read this, that is NOT a dig at you.) I'm in fear for my life as it is, so I cannot tell you who I am.[4]

Okay, so you're thinking, *But how*

[4] Editor's Note to Self: Absolutely remember to make sure that Mattie's name is not mentioned anywhere in this chapter. Not Mattie or his surname, Webmaker. Also remember to delete this footnote.

could demons possibly have destroyed your life? No one has seen a demon for ten thousand years. Well, I have. I have seen more than one. And I know more than I ever wanted to know. I'll get to that, I promise. But first I'll give you some background information about demons so you know what you need to know about the creatures we're talking about.

DEMONS & IMPS

Young demons are known as imps and have gray skin patterned with impressive glowing runes that spiral across their bodies. The runes increase and decrease in brightness and color according to the emotions the imp is feeling. Imps have wide flat noses, small eyes, and large sensitive ears.

An adult demon stands around five feet tall and is physically an entirely different entity than an imp. Their skin is a much darker gray and as tough as armor plating. They have a wide mouth full of incredibly sharp teeth. A demon's head is topped by a pair of magnificent horns formed by a series of bone ridges. And unlike the runic symbols that cover all of an imp's body, adult demons have only a trail of glowing runic symbols that decorate their chests and upper bodies. While the symbols don't cover the full body, they are certainly impressive and complete their ferocious, and rather frightening, appearance.

ORIGINS

Demons are different from all the other fairy races and have a unique evolutionary history. Sometime during the Triassic Period (around 199 to 251 million years ago), the moon was hit by a meteor, which broke off chunks of moon rock. One enormous piece fell to Earth, where it was fused into a magma stream and became part of the planet. This huge lump of moon rock became the island of Hybras.[5] Due to a combination of cosmic radiation and earthly magic, the lunar microorganisms that lay in hibernation inside the rock began to evolve at a greatly accelerated rate. Eventually, many millions of years later, they evolved into what we refer to today as demons.

[5] Editor's Note: Before it was sent to limbo, Hybras was located off the east coast of Ireland.

A TRUE AND CLASSIC IMAGE OF DEMON AS AN ADULT. NOTE THE GLOWING RUNIC SYMBOLS FOCUSED ACROSS THE CHEST AND UPPER ARMS AS WELL AS THE TELLTALE HORNS THAT INDICATE A FULLY GROWN ADULT DEMON.

LOST IN SPACE

Ten thousand years ago, the Fairy People faced a crisis. The surface was being overrun by Mud People. After the disastrous confrontation between fairy and human forces at the Battle of Taillte, all Fairy Folk were ordered by the Fairy Council to vacate the surface world and move belowground. Some lived in shallow forts near the surface; most moved deeper and set up the metropolis of Haven City.

The demons, however, were arrogant and refused to follow their fairy brethren to safety. The High Council of Demons decided on a plan to use magic to move the island of Hybras, where all demons lived, away from Earth entirely until it was safe to return.

A circle of demon warlocks cast a time spell over Hybras, with the intention of lifting it out of the time stream. To some degree, they succeeded. Hybras vanished from the face of the earth, and the island has never been seen again.

The Booke of the People describes how the time spell went horribly wrong. The warlocks could not control the powers they had unleashed. Hybras was cast into a timeless limbo and the warlocks were thrown off into space and killed. Without any living warlocks, the surviving demons could not return their island to real time and so have been trapped in limbo ever since.

The island is still magically linked with our dimension. Every now and then when the magical and planetary forces align, a demon finds themselves suddenly plucked from the island to appear on Earth for a few moments. It is incredibly hard to calculate when and where this might happen.

DEMON LIFE

Demons have a unique life cycle among the fairy races. Young demons, imps, are cute and approachable until the very moment they hit puberty. At that time, one of two things can happen. The imp metamorphoses into either a fully grown demon and loses all their magic, or the imp becomes a warlock, which looks physically like an imp but has increased magical abilities.

Imps who transform into demons usually do so around the age of twelve. Once the demonic hormones hit the young imp's system, the imp undergoes a violent spasm during which its pores begin to emit a green gunge. This process is extremely painful and

IMPS, OR YOUNG DEMONS, LOOK MUCH FRIENDLIER THAN THEIR GROWN-UP COUNTERPARTS, BUT BEAR IN MIND THEY ARE OFTEN JUST AS DANGEROUS.

several hours of loud high-pitched screaming is common. The gunge is actually high-nutrient slime and forms a cocoon around the imp similar to that of the caterpillars that make their home on the surface. The imp remains completely enveloped in this cocoon for between eight and ten hours. When the cocoon cracks open, the imp emerges in its adult form . . . a demon.

MOMMY DEAREST

Never known for being overly emotional, demons long ago did away with the bond between mothers and their children. The moment that a female demon lays an egg, it is snatched away and thrown rather harshly into a large bucket of very smelly mineral-enriched mud, where it stays until it hatches.[6] This means that newly hatched implings never get to know their family, or indeed, even who their family might be.

Because of this process, all demons are born equal. Their progress in life depends entirely on the strength of their teeth, claws, and character. In some ways this is a fair system, but if you are one of the smaller imps or demons, then it means that you are very much at the bottom of the heap and likely to remain there.

SCHOOL FOR IMPS

Young, pre-warp imps attend Imp School, a simple single-story stone building on Hybras. The classrooms inside have very little light or ventilation, making them hot and dark, just the way a young, pre-warp demon likes them. There's a saying that goes, "Children can be cruel," which by and large is true. There's another saying in demon society: "Demon children can be very cruel," which is even more true.

Subjects taught at Imp School include hunting, skinning, butchering, fighting, and studying, in extraordinary detail, the one single book that is in the school library: *Lady Heatherington Smythe's Hedgerow.*

BY THE BOOK

It is believed that demon society has suffered some strange changes while trapped in limbo on the now-timeless

[6] Editor's Note: And people complain about my childcare!

floating island of Hybras. Firstly, the demons have started eating rabbits. They never used to do that! Secondly, the whole of their society now revolves around the book *Lady Heatherington Smythe's Hedgerow*. Believe me, I know how that sounds and I wouldn't say it if it wasn't true.[7]

When the time spell was cast ten thousand years ago to make the island vanish, it had some weird side effects.

Lady Heatherington Smythe's Hedgerow is a romantic novel written by Carter Cooper Barbison. It is set at Heatherington Hall, and is about an English aristocrat. Noted in literary circles for its exceptional and frequent descriptions of woven herb-bread ropes, its minor success led to a flurry of bakery-oriented copycat books, the most famous of which is *Lord Glancington Bold's Gingerbits*.

One demon was randomly propelled into Earth time and appeared in the modern world for a few minutes. He had just enough time to pick up a copy of *Lady Heatherington Smythe's Hedgerow* before magical forces snatched him back to Hybras.

Believing that studying the book would help them defeat the Mud People in the next great battle, the demons pored over every word in the text. It quickly came to dominate their lives, with each imp being renamed as a character from the book as they transformed into demons. The book is required reading for all imps during their education, and they delight in quoting lines to each other, such as "Best foot forward, young sir, the world awaits." Which is ironic, as they are stuck in limbo and can't leave.

SECTION EIGHT, OR WHY I AM ON THE RUN

Until now, what I have been telling you is nothing new, for the most part. The information about the habits and history of demons can be found by those who choose to look for it in the archives of fairy history. But what I

[7] Editor's Note: You got that right, buddy.

IMPS AT IMP SCHOOL ARE TAUGHT BY A VARIETY OF HARSH AND CRUEL MASTERS, SUCH AS LORD SMEE SNOTSBERRY, WHERE THEY LEARN HARSH AND CRUEL LESSONS READY (IT'S SAID) FOR THEIR FUTURE HARSH AND CRUEL CONQUEST OF MUD PEOPLE. ME, I MUCH PREFER A WARMING CUP OF OAK ROOT TEA.

am *about* to tell you? The secrets I am *about* to reveal? Those are the ones that have nearly cost me my life. Be careful whom you talk to about them or they could cost you yours.

As the Fairy Folk of Haven City go about their daily business, none would even suspect the existence of Section Eight, a special organization dedicated to monitoring demons. Even L.E.P. officers will tell you that they have never heard of Section Eight, despite the fact that the shadowy organization started life as an offshoot of the L.E.P. many centuries ago. The job of Section Eight is to predict where and when demon manifestations may occur and ensure that such events do not endanger fairies by revealing their existence to Mud People.

I know this because I was a member of Section Eight. For over two years I served in this shadow organization. I did as I was told. I kept quiet. I told no one. Often, I asked those above me if we could bring to light the fact that, from time to time, demons do reappear. I thought the citizens of Haven City deserved to know. And time and time again I was overruled.

But I will remain silent no longer.

THE SECRET HISTORY OF SECTION EIGHT

Section Eight was created over five hundred years ago by Nan Burdeh, when she was chairman of the Fairy Council. She was (rightly) worried that a manifestation of a demon in the wrong place at the wrong time could result in the Fairy Folk's existence being exposed to the ever-warlike Mud People. So Burdeh spent decades secretly setting up Section Eight as a covert agency *within* an agency. Nan Burdeh was very rich, and when she died, she left her huge fortune to a trust dedicated to the continued funding of her brainchild.

The operatives of Section Eight wear uniforms of matte black and enjoy the use of some of the most sophisticated hardware in Haven City. Thanks to Nan Burdeh's fortune and the genius of carefully selected personnel from the L.E.P., the tech equipment of Section Eight is nearly a decade ahead of the L.E.P.'s standard issue. Shimmer Suits, high-tech helmets, multi-use communicators, and even their own hidden shuttleport all make Section Eight of a force to be reckoned with.

Over the long centuries since its creation, the brightest brains of Section Eight (often recruited from within the L.E.P. itself) have been struggling to achieve one crucial objective: the ability to accurately predict exactly where and when demon manifestations will occur. They need to be able to ensure no human ever sees one, or perhaps more accurately, that no human ever *remembers* one. If a demon were to materialize in front of a camera-carrying crowd of Mud Men, or even worse, be captured, then the whole of fairy civilization would be at risk.

I'm risking my freedom and possibly my life going public with this. Maybe if everyone knows about Section Eight, I can stop running and get my life back. Maybe.

CHAPTER
11

CENTAURS

CENTAURS ARE KNOWN AS THE BRAINS OF THE FAIRY FAMILY, AND THERE'S NO DENYING THAT THEY ARE EXTREMELY SMART. SOME OF THE MOST IMPORTANT TECHNOLOGICAL DEVELOPMENTS IN RECENT YEARS HAVE BEEN INVENTED BY CENTAURS. AND IT'S THAT CENTAUR-DEVELOPED TECH THAT HAS ENSURED THAT HAVEN CITY CONTINUES TO GO UNNOTICED BY MUD PEOPLE. OUR MAIN FEATURE IN THIS CHAPTER IS AN EXCLUSIVE INTERVIEW WITH THE L.E.P.'S RESIDENT GENIUS, FOALY.[1] AS USUAL, WE WILL BEGIN OUR EXPLORATION WITH OUR SPOTTER'S GUIDE. . . .

SPOTTER'S GUIDE — CENTAURS

SPECIES: Centaur. Two subspecies made up of unicorn and pegasus.

LOOKS LIKE: Half-humanoid, half-horse. Don't confuse them with unicorns. They hate that!

SIZE: Thanks to their horsey lower half, centaurs stand pretty tall, especially in the fairy world.

PERSONALITY: Smart. Some people say *too* smart. There's no doubt about their intelligence, but they can also be arrogant and aloof. Centaurs have a tendency to overthink things and can easily become paranoid.

MOST LIKELY TO BE CAUGHT DOING: Something brainy to a complex piece of advanced technology.

MOST EASILY SPOTTED WHEN: They walk by and you accidentally get whacked by a horse's tail.

[1] Editor's Note: Foaly informed me he was "far too busy to write for a book like this," which he says "represents everything about dumbed-down publishing." Anyway, I sent along this Moonpad kid who's desperate to break into publishing and said he'd work for free. He did a great job with the interview and a swell job vacuuming my office afterward.

Encrypted Message

Butler,

What schoolboy hasn't gazed at the mosaic *Battle of Centaurs and Wild Beasts* on the wall of Roman emperor Hadrian's villa retreat in wonder?[2] Actually, probably most of them, Butler, since by and large my classmates seem to be more interested in football and watching the new episodes of *I Have a Sob Story, So Make Me a Teenage Pop Star*, or *IHASSSMMATPS*, as they insist on calling it for short.

My classmates' lack of culture aside, centaurs were part of Greek—and later, Roman—mythology for thousands of years. The image of a creature that is half-human and half-horse is a powerful one, and there are many depictions of the creatures in classical art. (All of which, it goes without saying, have gone unstudied by my classmates, but I suppose I must learn to let that go.)

Human scholars have suggested that the idea for centaurs came from people seeing riders on horseback for the first time and mistakenly believing that they were one creature. Honestly . . . I know not everyone can be a genius like me, but how dim can you be to make that mistake?[3] You and I, Butler, know that like so many other legends, centaurs are very real. They are said to be the smartest of all the Fairy Folk, although obviously still NOT as smart as me. The enclosed file contains various strategies for outsmarting and removing certain centaurs should it ever become necessary to do so. Please read and digest.

AF II

---

[2] Editor's Note: Excuse me while I doze off. . . . *Zzzzzzz*.

[3] Editor's Note: The Fowl kid and Foaly were made for each other. Each one thinks the other is a show-off, and for once, they're both right!

I THINK CENTAURS AND TUNNEL DWARFS GET ALONG SO WELL BECAUSE WE ARE BOTH FAMED FOR OUR INTELLECTUAL BRAIN-TYPE CAPABILITIES. EVERYONE IN HAVEN CITY KNOWS THAT YOU CAN NEVER HOPE TO OUTSMART A CENTAUR OR A DWARF. THE ONLY DIFFERENCE BETWEEN US IS THAT AS WELL AS BEING REALLY SMART IN THE HEAD, DWARFS ALSO HAVE EXTRAORDINARY TUNNELING SKILLS THAT CENTAURS LACK, AND, ON TOP OF ALL THOSE THINGS, WE DWARFS ARE VERY MODEST, TOO.

WHEN YOUR OLD PAL MULCH DIGGUMS THINKS ABOUT CENTAURS, ONE FACE COMES TO MIND... FOALY, OR AS I LIKE TO CALL HIM, "PONY BOY." I CAN'T RECALL HOW MANY TIMES EITHER FOALY OR ONE OF HIS INVENTIONS HELPED THE L.E.P. FRAME ME FOR SOME CRIME I DIDN'T COMMIT AND COULDN'T HAVE COMMITTED EVEN IF I WANTED TO BECAUSE I WAS DEFINITELY SOMEWHERE ELSE AT THE TIME.

WAYS FOALY HAS TRIED TO FRAME ME FOR CRIMES THAT I DID NOT DO:

1. HIDING STOLEN STUFF IN MY CAVE AND THEN BUSTING IN WITH A SEARCH WARRANT.
2. LEAVING MY BUM PRINT AT THE SCENE OF A CRIME.
3. PAYING SOMEONE WHO LOOKS LIKE ME (LUCKY GUY!) TO WALK AROUND IN FRONT OF CCTV CAMERAS JUST BEFORE A CRIME IS COMMITTED.
4. MOST OUTRAGEOUSLY OF ALL, TRICKING ME INTO CHECKING INTO A FANCY LUXURY EIGHTEEN-STAR HOTEL AND SPENDING MONEY FROM A CRIME I DIDN'T COMMIT.

DESPITE ALL THE TERRIBLE THINGS LISTED ABOVE THAT FOALY HAS TRIED TO DO TO ME, I REGARD HIM AS A PERSONAL FRIEND. HE IS ONE OF ONLY A HANDFUL OF PEOPLE THAT I CONSIDER TO BE NEARLY AS SMART AS I AM.

MULCH

FOALY IS THE GENIUS BEHIND MUCH OF THE L.E.P.'S CRIME-FIGHTING TECHNOLOGY AND IS ALSO CREDITED WITH HELPING KEEP THE EXISTENCE OF FAIRIES HIDDEN FROM THE MUD PEOPLE. THE FACT THAT HE IS RESPONSIBLE FOR SO MUCH L.E.P. TECH MAKES HIM ONE OF THE MOST POPULAR AND UNPOPULAR FAIRIES IN HAVEN CITY, DEPENDING ON WHICH SIDE OF THE LAW YOU ARE ON. WE SENT OUR PROFESSIONAL INTERVIEWING INTERN,[4] SCRATCH MOONPAD, TO TALK TO HIM.

DOUBLE LIFE: MY INTERVIEW WITH FOALY

By SCRATCH MOONPAD

FOALY: You look a little nervous. You all right?

MOONPAD: Absolutely fine. I've done many, many interviews.

FOALY: Really?

MOONPAD: No. Not really. But let's not dwell on it. Centaurs. What can you tell me?

FOALY: Centaurs are half humanoid and half horse. Certain dwarf friends of mine are always asking, "Oh, which half is which?" But for a centaur it's no laughing matter. There are fewer of us centaurs than almost any other fairy species, like elves or pixies, so we tend to be a bit sensitive about—

MOONPAD: Everything?

FOALY: No, not everything! Just things to do with being a centaur, and everything else not to do with being a centaur. Just those two things.

MOONPAD: Right. Okay. Moving on. What's life like as a centaur?

FOALY: You looking for a "life on

[4] Editor's Note: I.e., that kid who hangs around the office.

the hoof" joke? Centaurs are rightly known for their superior intelligence. We don't have any magic, but we have brainpower. Everyone says that we're paranoid.

MOONPAD: Not everyone. Some people.

FOALY: No, it's everyone. It's what they're thinking all the time. It's what they talk about when they think we're not looking. "Look at the centaur over there, bet he's paranoid," they whisper behind our backs. You don't hear people saying that unicorns are paranoid, do you?

MOONPAD: Er . . . well, no.

FOALY: And do you know why? Because there are none left. They went extinct because they didn't believe people were out to get them. Boy, were they wrong, and that's a lesson for you right there!

UNICORNS

Unicorns are now extinct. Gone. No more. They are truly just the stuff of legend. But while they are gone, they should not be forgotten. Instead, they should serve as a reminder to all the fairy races of what can happen when your existence becomes common knowledge among Mud People.

Unicorns were the cousins of the centaurs, and for centuries, the two species coexisted and formed powerful bonds. A unicorn was a white horse with a single large magical horn projecting from its forehead. Unlike centaurs, the unicorns were a carefree species that was happy to interact with ancient mankind.

Unfortunately, Mud Men took advantage of this naïveté and hunted the unicorn for the magical properties of its horn, which they rightly believed would heal sickness and make poisoned water drinkable. Tragically, unicorns were hunted to extinction by Mud Men, an event that left the centaurs more paranoid and nervous than ever.[5] Ironically, unicorns came to represent purity and grace to the Mud People, while to centaurs they represent, well, you know, death.

---

[5] Editor's Note: Unless you believe the rumors about . . . you know. . . . But I've said too much.

MOONPAD: So, um, can you tell me about Centaurian? Is it really the oldest form of writing in the world?

FOALY: Of course. It's not at all surprising that centaurs invented writing before anyone else. We're brilliant, remember? We've been writing for ten thousand years.

MOONPAD: Wow. Your hands must be really tired.

FOALY: This is serious.

MOONPAD: Sorry.

FOALY: There are, at most, half a dozen of us who can read ancient Centaurian. Not that a lot of the old writing still exists. To date, only one of the Scrolls of Capalla survives. Though, given our brilliance, I imagine it is only a matter of time before we uncover more texts.

EXCERPT FROM THE LAST SURVIVING SCROLL OF CAPALLA

Fairy creatures, heed this warning,
On Earth, the human era is dawning.
So hide, fairy, lest you be found,
And make a home beneath the ground.

Take the classic verse from the scrolls that begins "Fairy creatures, heed this warning . . ." Here the ancient centaurs are speaking to us down through the centuries with a timeless lesson. They're reminding us that Mud People and Fairy Folk do not mix well. Although fairies have magic—or sheer brilliance, in some cases—on our side, there are just too many of the Mud People. They are aggressive, greedy, and have no morals. Just look at what they're doing to the surface! They're polluting the oceans, cutting down the forests, and raising the overall temperature of the atmosphere. We have to make sure that Haven City, and fairies everywhere, remain hidden from Mud People.

MOONPAD: I had no idea the scrolls were so . . . prophetic.

FOALY: Of course. Why would you? You aren't a centaur. It would be too much for your small brain to process.

MOONPAD: Oh. Um, okay. Well, anyway . . . You are credited as being one of Haven City's main protectors, keeping us safe with your technology and ensuring we are not discovered

CENTAURS ARE EASILY FRIGHTENED. THEY “SPOOK” AT THE SMALLEST OF OBJECTS. EVEN SPIDERS SEND THEM RUNNING. WHICH IS SILLY, AS WHAT COULD A SPIDER DO TO A HORSE?

CENTAURS ARE NATURAL INVENTORS AND ENGINEERS. THEY ARE HIGHLY DISCIPLINED IN THEIR THINKING AND, LIKE DWARFS, HAVE A WONDERFUL WORK ETHIC.

by the Mud People for all the reasons that you just mentioned. Do you worry about being spied on by the Mud People's intelligence agencies?

FOALY: Look, all it would take to expose our entire civilization to the Mud People is one stray goblin wandering through a city center and getting photographed. One troll breaking the surface near a Mud Person city. Or a pair of Hummingbird wings failing and dumping an L.E.P. elf somewhere they don't want to be. That's all it would take, because once humans know we exist, they'll start digging around and the troll dung will hit the fan. So if I take steps to protect myself and create tech that keeps us hidden, then that's not something I'm embarrassed about. I'm proud of it.

MOONPAD: Fair point.

FOALY: Although if you wanted to cut that out of the interview, that would be fine, too.

MOONPAD: We'll consider it. Moving on . . . What are the more difficult parts of being a centaur?

FOALY: Well, I wouldn't want to speak for all centaurs. It's not like I'm some highly regarded, well-thought-of, super-successful genius, saving lives with my brilliant technological inventions every day.

What I *will* say is that being a centaur isn't always easy. We're some of the smartest fairies under the planet, but from the waist down I'm a horse. You see what I mean? It's not the extra expense of two pairs of shoes, or even the vat of shampoo for my tail. It's just not always easy being half animal. You get some odd instincts. Sometimes I'm drawn to apples. And I don't even like apples. I see a fence and I want to jump it. I see a little bug or spider and the horse bit of me freaks out.

MOONPAD: Really?

FOALY: Just for a second. And you know, not so you'd notice.

MOONPAD: Can you tell me how centaur society works?

FOALY: What?

MOONPAD: You know, goblins have their street gangs, and dwarfs have their secret underground brotherhoods. You . . . okay?

FOALY: Listen . . . it breaks my heart to say this aloud, but there aren't really enough centaurs left to have a society. Most of my best friends are elves and, as much as I hate to admit it, dwarfs. If I meet a centaur I don't already know in the course of my day, that's really unusual. It's nice. It's lovely, in fact, but it's a real surprise. There's just not that many of us. We're like those lone wolves up on the surface. Stick to ourselves, mostly because we don't have a choice. So joking aside, you might think we're a touch paranoid, but we've got good reason to be. Hunting by humans decimated my people, and we've never recovered.

MOONPAD: I'm so sorry, Foaly. I never thought of it that way.

FOALY: Got a bit serious there,

TOP TEN FOALY INVENTIONS

10. **CAM-FOIL**—sheet that makes the wearer practically invisible.
9. **MIND-WIPE**—deletes memories. Used on Mud People who have seen a fairy.
8. **PEEP PLOTTER**—a program that documents the movements of all the criminals implanted with a tracker device.
7. **NEUTRINO 500, 2000, AND 3000 SERIES OF HANDGUNS**—settings allow the stunning of nearly all life-forms, thus saving lives.
6. **RETIMAGER**—a unique piece of tech that retrieves the last image seen from the surface of an eyeball.
5. **SENTINEL**—sophisticated computer system which monitors all human digital communications looking for fairy-related key words.
4. **MOOD BLANKET**—this multi-sensor massage garment was invented especially for centaurs.
3. **LUNAR PANELS**—secret project to capture moonlight on the surface and pipe it underground, enabling the fairy recharging Ritual to be completed in safety.
2. **DART FINGER**—worn on top of an actual finger, it fires a single dart full of tranquilizer.
1. **TIME-FREEZE TECHNOLOGY**—This needs a proper explanation:

A time-stop is a delicate procedure that is only used by the L.E.P. in the most dire of circumstances. It involves placing didn't I? Sorry about that. I'm not old enough to remember the ancient times. Great herds of centaurs living in a peaceful society, talking, debating, thinking, and inventing together. That was all lost before we were forced underground by Mud People.

MOONPAD: That must be a terrible weight to carry around.

FOALY: It's okay. Thanks, I guess. I mean, it's just nice to know that someone cares.

MOONPAD: Of course. So, out of all your inventions . . . what's your favorite?

a series of five signal dishes around a chosen area and then transmitting warlock magic to create a bubble around the area that freezes it in time (and that includes all individuals within that space). Due to the instabilities created when freezing the time and space continuum, time-stops have a maximum length of eight hours.

The practice goes back thousands of years and was traditionally performed by the five most powerful warlocks of the day. The success of any time-stop used to depend on all five warlocks keeping their concentration and not needing the bathroom for several hours. A warlock's concentration was often more reliable than their bladder, and many a time-stop came to a chaotic end when a warlock had to rush to the restroom. One such collapsed time-stop resulted in a village in the highlands of Scotland that now only appears for one day out of every hundred years. Time is a funny thing.

Foaly's great leap forward in time-stop technology was to persuade warlocks to store their power in battery form, making it available whenever needed in a controllable and reliable form. This simple innovation proved a game changer for the reliability of time-stops. Foaly's battery tech is credited with having saved the People several times.

Before Mud People developed computer technology, all time-stops on the surface went unnoticed. With the invention of satellites and instantaneous communications, time-stops are more likely to be spotted and so are only used in emergency situations.

FOALY: If I had to pick just one of my brilliant inventions . . . I would be tempted to say the iris-cam, because that won me a prize at my college science fair, but that would be showing off. So I'll just say my favorite invention is the time-freeze. That amazing device has saved the whole of fairy civilization on more than one occasion.

But since we don't have a time-stop going on in here, kid, I have to go. I've had twenty-seven brilliant ideas for new inventions while I've been talking to you, and I need to write them down.

MOONPAD: I've inspired you?

FOALY: Kind of . . . I often get my best ideas while bored and talking to people who are my intellectual inferiors. I've had a load of ideas today, so thank you.

MOONPAD: Er . . . my pleasure. I think. Did you just insult me?

FOALY: Absolutely not.

MOONPAD: Okay, thanks.

FOALY: Just stating the facts.

MOONPAD: Could you take me through how some of your most famous L.E.P. equipment works?

FOALY: Listen, young fellow, it's been a real spirit-raiser talking about extinction, death, and loneliness with you, but I have to get back to work. But I'll tell you what. I'll give you an introduction to the man who uses all the tech. Our chief training officer.

MOONPAD: Does he like talking to people?

FOALY: No, he hates it. But he never gets any credit, so you go flatter his ego and see if he'll talk. You're getting paid for doing this, right?

MOONPAD: Er . . . not exactly. The way it works is . . .

[RECORDING ABRUPTLY ENDS]

CHAPTER 12

FAIRY TECHNOLOGY

OKAY, SO IT'S NOT A SPECIES, BUT NO SELF-RESPECTING GUIDE TO THE WORLD OF THE FAIRY FOLK WOULD FEEL COMPLETE WITHOUT TAKING A CLOSE LOOK AT SOME L.E.P. TECHNOLOGY. WE'RE ALL VERY LUCKY THAT THE FAIRY PEOPLE WERE GIFTED WITH BRAINS AND NOT JUST MAGIC. OUR TECH IS LIGHT-YEARS AHEAD OF THE MUD PEOPLE ON THE SURFACE, AND JUST AS WELL, BECAUSE WE NEED IT TO BE ABLE TO HIDE FROM THEM.

FOR A GUIDED TOUR OF THE L.E.P.'S FINEST EQUIPMENT, WE WENT TO THE GNOME WHO TEACHES CADETS HOW TO USE IT, CHIEF TRAINING OFFICER PAYE TENTION.

BUT FIRST, OUR SPOTTER'S GUIDE.

SPOTTER'S GUIDE — FAIRY TECHNOLOGY

LOOKS LIKE: Something from the year 2066.

SIZE: Varies. Usually small and neat.

PERSONALITY: Inventive.

MOST LIKELY TO BE CAUGHT DOING: What's best to keep Haven City safe.

MOST EASILY SPOTTED WHEN: You see it being expertly used in the hands of an L.E.P. officer.

Encrypted Message

Butler:

I've discovered that perhaps the most amazing thing of all is not the Fairy People themselves, but their technology.

We have the very latest developments in spy tech, Butler, but this fairy equipment is far more advanced than anything that humans have. If we could get some more samples of fairy equipment to dismantle, I'm sure someone with my vast intellectual capacity could discover how it works and replicate it.

You know how much I enjoyed building that digital-safecracker last year? And how effective it proved to be in the field? (Even if you did make me give all the proceeds from our successful test run to the school charity.) That would be nothing in comparison with what I could do with technology developed by the fairies. With fairy tech at our disposal, the sky would be the limit!

AF II

AH, L.E.P. TECHNOLOGY. I DON'T MIND ADMITTING THAT I HAVE A KINDA LOVE-HATE RELATIONSHIP WITH L.E.P. TECHNOLOGY. I LOVE STEALING IT, BUT I HATE WHEN THEY USE IT TO CATCH ME.

IT GOES WITHOUT MENTION—BUT JUST IN CASE YOU DON'T KNOW, I'LL MENTION IT NOW—THAT I JUST HAPPEN TO BE PRETTY MUCH BEST BUDDIES WITH THE BRAIN THAT INVENTED ALL THE BEST FAIRY GADGETS. I WON'T DROP ANY NAMES HERE, BUT LET'S JUST SAY HE HAS FOUR HOOVES AND A NAME THAT SOUNDS A BIT HORSEY.

A LOT OF L.E.P. TECH WAS DESIGNED WITH CATCHING CRIMINALS IN MIND, SO IT'S NOT EXACTLY MY FAVORITE THING IN THE WHOLE WORLD (EVEN IF MY BESTIE MAKES IT). BUT IF I DID HAVE TO PICK ONE PIECE I HATE LESS THAN THE OTHERS, THEN I GUESS IT WOULD BE CAM-FOIL. IT COMES IN SHEETS THAT ARE EACH ABOUT THE SIZE OF A GOBLIN AND IS COATED WITH SOME KINDA MAGIC TECH PARTICLES (HEY, LOOK, I NEVER SAID I UNDERSTOOD HOW THIS STUFF WORKS) THAT MAKES YOU PRACTICALLY INVISIBLE WHEN YOU PUT IT OVER YOURSELF.[1]

ANYHOW, I THINK YOU MIGHT BE ABLE TO IMAGINE HOW BEING NEARLY INVISIBLE MIGHT BE HANDY IN MY LINE OF WORK. (NOT THAT IT WOULD BE FAIR TO DEPRIVE THE WORLD OF MY HANDSOME FEATURES FOR VERY LONG.)[2] IF YOU'RE THINKING OF USING THE CAM-FOIL, ONE PIECE OF ADVICE: REMEMBER THAT GUARD DOGS CAN STILL SMELL YOU EVEN THOUGH YOU'RE INVISIBLE. I KNOW THAT'S TRUE FROM PAINFUL PERSONAL EXPERIENCE. (OUCH, MY POOR BEHIND!)[3]

MULCH

---

[1] Editor's Note: Advanced microcircuitry analyzes the wearer's background and then displays it on the front of the cam-foil, making them pretty much invisible. So I'm told, anyway.

[2] Editor's Note: We'll survive.

[3] Editor's Note: If anyone out there has CCTV footage of Mulch and the guard dogs, please send it in to me. It's not for the book. I could just do with a laugh.

PAYE TENTION IS THE CHIEF TRAINING OFFICER AT THE RENOWNED L.E.P. ACADEMY. HE DESCRIBES HIMSELF AS "THAT BIG HAIRY GNOME WHO PINS EACH CADET TO A WALL ON THEIR FIRST DAY OF TRAINING AND WARNS THEM NEVER TO RUN INTO AN UNSECURED BUILDING DURING A FIREFIGHT. THAT'S ME, AND I'M PROUD OF THAT." HE IS ALSO KEENLY AWARE OF THE IMPORTANCE OF EACH PIECE OF TECH IN THE L.E.P. ARSENAL AND THE BENEFITS/DANGERS OF SAID TECH.

FOR SAFEKEEPING: FAIRY TECH AND ITS USES

By PAYE TENTION

Instructor Tention warned us that he didn't have time to write an article about fairy technology for this book, but thanks to some sweet-talking from Foaly, he did agree to be interviewed. Therefore, an unedited transcript of the interview with elf reporter Scratch Moonpad is presented below.[4] They met in the L.E.P. Academy training building.

CHIEF TRAINING OFFICER TENTION: I'm not writing anything down. I told Foaly that.

MOONPAD: I know.

INSTRUCTOR TENTION: Nothing.

MOONPAD: I understand.

INSTRUCTOR TENTION: You wanna ask me questions, sure, I'll answer 'em. But I ain't writing nothing down. You have any idea how many training reports I have to type every week for the L.E.P.?

MOONPAD: Er . . . no, I don't.

INSTRUCTOR TENTION: None, 'cuz I don't do it. I just give the kids a verbal grade. But if I did do it, it would

[4] Editor's Note: I.e., that kid who hangs around the office.

be an awful lot, you better believe me. Sure, they're always saying, "Oh, Chief Training Officer Tention, we need a full written report on this and a full assessment-test appraisal on that." But you know what? As I stand here this morning, I am forty-three years behind on my paperwork, so it doesn't look like I'm gonna catch up anytime soon.

[A PAUSE. AND THE SOUND OF MOONPAD SHIFTING UNCOMFORTABLY IN HIS SEAT CAN BE HEARD ON THE TAPE]

INSTRUCTOR TENTION: You got one hour, kid, then I'm kicking you outta here, whether you're Foaly's little pal or not. So, what's your first question?

MOONPAD: It's . . .

INSTRUCTOR TENTION: I'll tell you your first question. It's "What's my name?" That should be your first question. My name is Paye Tention, and I'm the chief training officer for the entire L.E.P. Academy. You think it's Foaly who's the brains of this place? You think it's Commander Root who makes this place tick? You're wrong on both counts. It's me, Officer Tention. I've overseen the training of every L.E.P. officer in the Academy for the last century. The L.E.P. Academy ticks because I make it tick.[5]

MOONPAD: Really?

INSTRUCTOR TENTION: Why, sure, kid. But maybe don't put that bit in your article in case the higher-ups get their noses all out of joint hearing the truth. You can just say I'm a little cog in a big machine. Sure, it's true that without this little cog the entire machine around it would completely fall apart and fail to function, but let's not dwell on that.

[SOUND OF PAPER UNWRAPPING AND THE UNMISTAKABLE SOUND OF CHEWING]

So, where do you wanna start?

MOONPAD: Well, as we're here to talk about fairy technology, could we please start with, say, the standard-issue neutrino gun?

INSTRUCTOR TENTION: No.

MOONPAD: No?

INSTRUCTOR TENTION: Yes, no. I

[5] Editor's Note: I felt like there should have been a clock gag here, but I couldn't think of one in time. (Time, geddit? Honestly, I'm wasted behind the scenes.)

figure, seeing as we're just by the chute bays, we'll start with transport to the surface.

So, say a gang of goblins starts terrorizing a deserted farmhouse at night, scaring a family of Mud People, and the L.E.P. needs to get those green-skinned goofballs back underground quickly. How do we get officers from L.E.P.recon, the elite branch of the Lower Elements Police, up to the surface in time to stop those fire-loving freaks exposing our existence to Mud People? you ask.

MOONPAD: A pressure elevator?

INSTRUCTOR TENTION: You got it, kid! We put the officer into a titanium egg and shoot them to the surface in a pressure elevator on a natural current of hot magma. The officer rides safely inside the egg, protected from the incredible heat. The egg is lifted by a venting flow of magma and carried up to the surface at an extremely high speed. Impressive, right?[6]

MOONPAD: Very. How safe is it?

INSTRUCTOR TENTION: It's 100 percent safe. Everybody gets exactly where they need to be with 100 percent safety and no fatalities or accidents. When I say 100 percent, I obviously mean about 99.8 percent. You have to factor in the odd magma mishap, of course.

MOONPAD: Don't people worry about that 0.2 percent?

INSTUCTOR TENTION: Worry about the pressure cracking their heads open

BLUE RINSE—informal slang term for a bio-bomb. A biological weapon that is only used in times of extreme danger to the People. The bomb kills all living things while leaving their nonliving surroundings untouched. In its core is a radioactive element, solinium 2, that has a half-life of fourteen seconds. It was invented by the centaur Foaly, and it is widely rumored that he has regretted it ever since.

[6] Editor's Note: Impressive, but bumpy as heck. Take it from me, I've done it.

like a troll stamping on an egg? Worry about their old gray matter ending up as interior decoration for the pod? Nah. What's the point? If that were to happen, it would be over before you knew what was going on.

MOONPAD: [GULPS]

INSTRUCTOR TENTION: Look, kid, Recon is a notoriously dangerous job. Really dangerous. These brave officers are putting their lives on the line for Haven City every single day. The fatality rate in a firefight with a goblin gang or a face-off with troll smugglers is much higher than when you're sitting inside a big metal egg being bumped along by magma. You wanna look inside?

MOONPAD: Yeah, sure.

[SOUND OF A CHAIR SCREECHING AND FOOTSTEPS; THE SOUND QUALITY GROWS WEAKER]

INSTRUCTOR TENTION: Inside, there is enough room for a restraining seat so our officer can be safely strapped in. In front, you see, there's a few controls. These eggs are designed to be blasted along by the magma, but there is a small engine in the rear, so once the pod reaches the surface it can be maneuvered by thrusters to where the officer needs to be. This little beauty has been engulfed in magma at regular intervals for the last fifty years, and she's still going strong.

[SOUND OF HAND BANGING ON METAL]

Okay, let's go and look at the field equipment.

[RECORDER CLICKS OFF]
[RECORDER CLICKS BACK ON]

MOONPAD: We are back at L.E.P. Academy with Instructor Tention, who has—

INSTRUCTOR TENTION: Why do you have to say all that? We know where we are. Anyway, you want to learn more or not?

MOONPAD: Of course, sir. I'm so sorry, sir.

INSTRUCTOR TENTION: The L.E.P. have regular aerial patrols all over Haven City. They cover everything from monitoring traffic flow to responding to emergency situations. Many of our Flying Squad are sprites who have natural wings, so where possible we use

WINGS

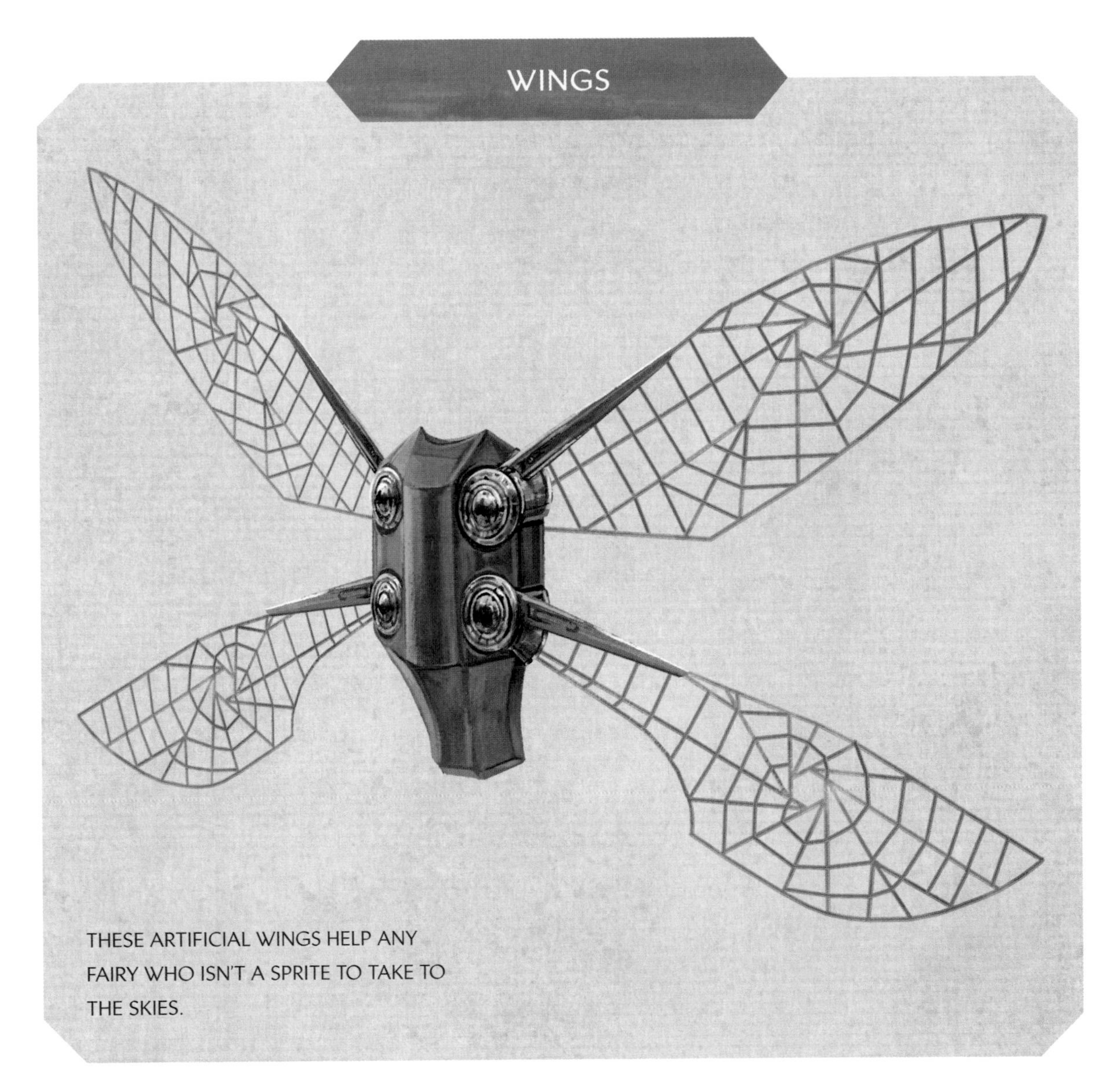

THESE ARTIFICIAL WINGS HELP ANY FAIRY WHO ISN'T A SPRITE TO TAKE TO THE SKIES.

them for aerial patrols. When we do, we need to limit their time in the air so that they don't overtax their flying abilities. That said, I don't know a sprite who wouldn't rather be in the air than walking. When fairy officers who are not naturally winged are on airborne patrol, they have a number of mechanical-wing options. We have Dragonflies, an older, heavier model with a petrol engine. There's also our new wings, the Hummingbird Z7. Those bad boys are as silent as a breeze, and are powered by solar batteries with enough juice to

NEUTRINO 2000

SOME MUD PEOPLE MISTAKE THESE SWEET LITTLE GADGETS FOR CUTE TOYS. BUT JOKE'S ON THEM. THE NEUTRINO GUN PACKS A SERIOUS PUNCH!

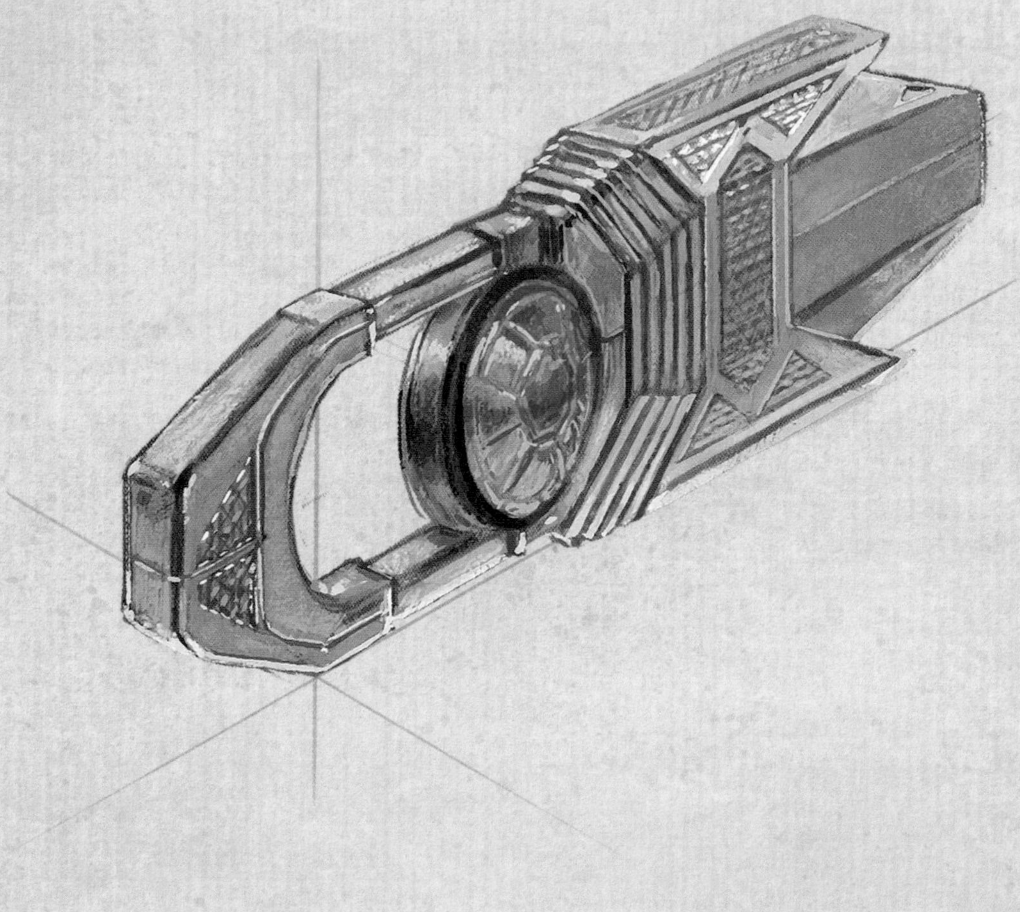

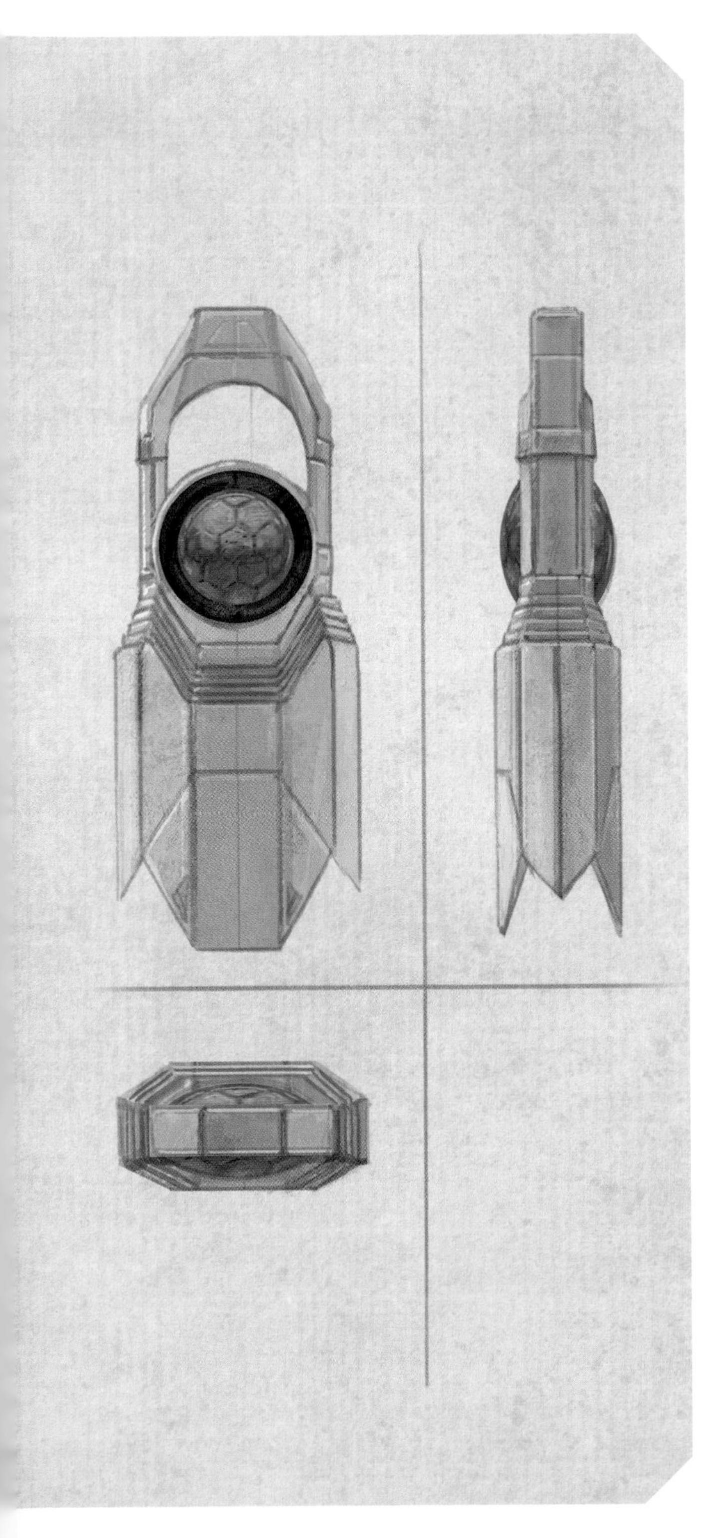

fly you around the world twice. My officers love them.

MOONPAD: Have you tried them yourself?

INSTRUCTOR TENTION: There's a weight limit. Let's move on.

MOONPAD: What can you tell me about the specialized equipment?

INSTRUCTOR TENTION: There's the iris-cam. You heard of that? It's a teeny, tiny miniaturized camera that fits neatly over the iris in your eye. Get it? Iris-cam? Anyway, you going undercover in Goblin Town? You slip one of these beauties in your eye and L.E.P. Control can see and record everything that you see. They can help officers in the field by switching to magnification mode or heat vision mode. Little thing can be kind of a problem. Causes irritation in the eye if an officer uses one for too long. And they cost a crock of gold as well, so we don't have many.

MOONPAD: Who invented the iris-cam?

INSTRUCTOR TENTION: You already know the answer to that one, kid. Our resident tech genius, Foaly, is responsible for most of this stuff.

MOONPAD: That's what he said. Just checking.

INSTRUCTOR TENTION: You see this?

MOONPAD: An ear? Ugh! Is it real?

INSTRUCTOR TENTION: Of course it's not real. You think I walk around here with elf ears in my pockets? We call this the All Ears. Officers slip them on over the tops of their real ears, and not only can we hear everything that they can hear, but we can deliver messages to them without anyone else hearing.

MOONPAD: So it's perfect for undercover work?

INSTRUCTOR TENTION: You got it. Now, take a look at these. This is the Neutrino series of weapons. The Neutrino 500 is a light handgun. It has various nonfatal settings to enable officers to bring down perps. The Neutrino 2000 is the cream of the crop. This blaster has a platinum outer coating and is powered by tiny nuclear batteries that will outlive your grandkids. It has three settings for firepower. I used to call them one, two, and three—original, huh? But the guys have their own pet names for them. Setting one is scorched, two is well-done, and three is crisped to a cinder. Someone hit by a level-three blast is going to be unconscious for around eight hours.

MOONPAD: Ouch.[7]

INSTRUCTOR TENTION: I won't lie to you: You get zapped by this, and it's gonna sting in the morning like the headache from a goblin wedding. The 2000 is versatile and reliable, which is why it's our standard-issue weapon of choice for patrolling Haven City.

[SOUND OF MORE FOOTSTEPS AND A LOUD GRUNT AS SOMEONE RUNS INTO AN OBJECT]

INSTRUCTOR TENTION: Okay, next up we have this beauty of classic design . . . the L.E.P.recon helmet. If you're assigned to the field, then chances are you're wearing one of these.

MOONPAD: For protection?

INSTRUCTOR TENTION: Partly for protection, but this helmet can do a heap more than cover your head. For a start, it has a tracking system built in, so L.E.P. Control can tell where you are at all times. It also has a filter mask, which can save your life if there's gas or Mud People pollution around. It has

[7] Editor's Note: Yeah, ouch!

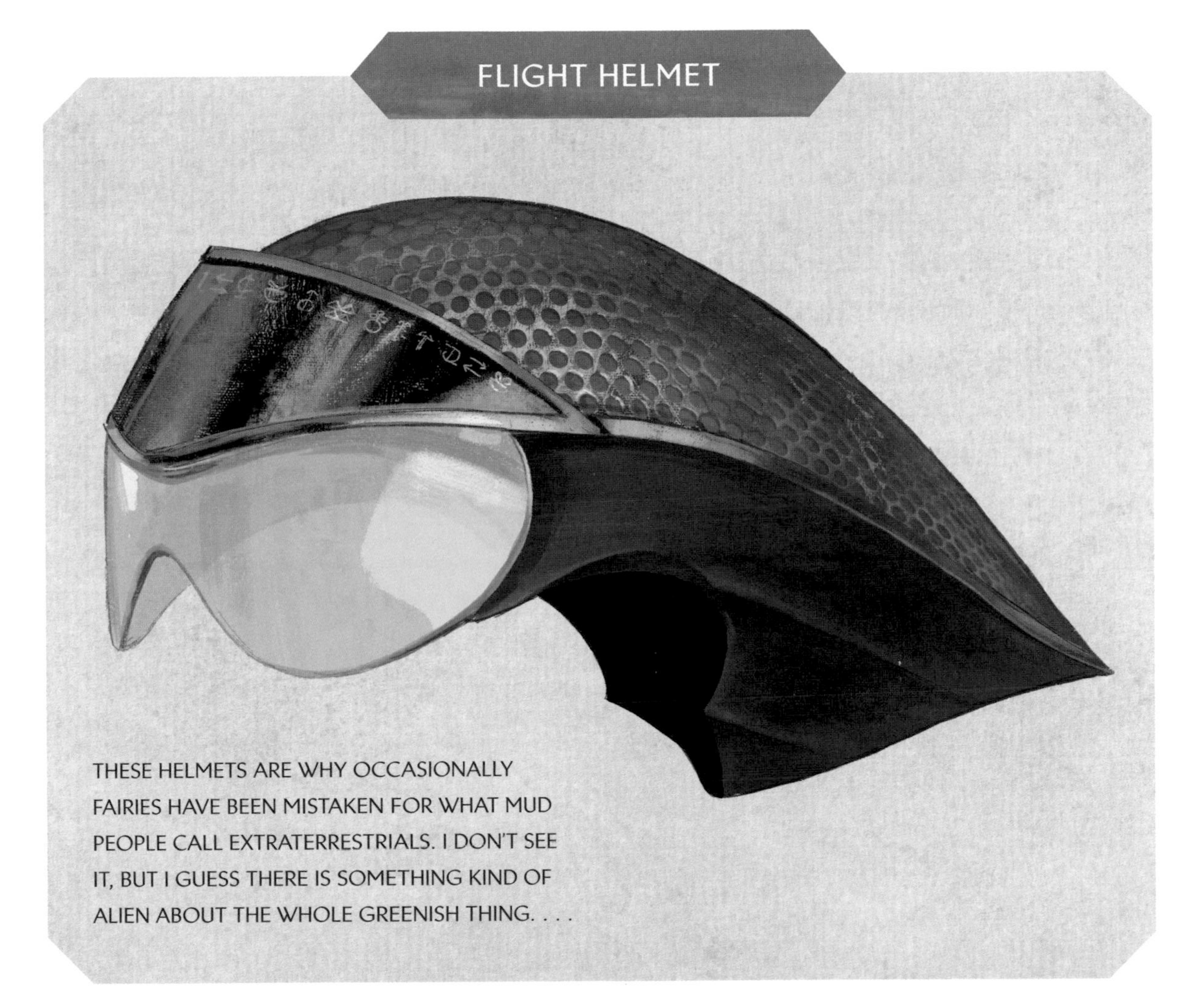

an eye screen that has more visual filters than I have fingers.

MOONPAD: Filters?

INSTRUCTOR TENTION: So, it's got infrared, thermal imaging, night vision, anti-shield vision, and argonsight. If you're working a shift on the surface for L.E.P.recon and you need to be shielded to prevent any Mud Men from seeing you or, even worse, getting a photograph of you, the helmet is your best friend. But it gets more impressive. Because here's the thing: You also need to be able to see your fellow officers, or you might fly straight into them. The anti-shield function means that even if they have their shields engaged and are invisible to the naked eye, you can look through your helmet visor and see them as clear as you can see me right now.

MOONPAD: Wow.

INSTRUCTOR TENTION: Yeah, wow. All the functions are voice-activated, so the officer has his or her hands free at all times. It has its own lighting beams for use in tunnels or with trolls. Also, it looks very darn cool.

MOONPAD: Yeah, it sure does. Do you think I could try one on?

INSTRUCTOR TENTION: NO! This is a piece of incredibly expensive and delicate professional equipment!

MOONPAD: Oh, sorry.

INSTRUCTOR TENTION: I'm just messing with you, kid. 'Course you can.

[RECORDING PAUSES AGAIN]

INSTRUCTOR TENTION: Well, that's it, kid. That's your hour. I gotta get back to my rookies' class on buzz batons before those ten thousand volts go somewhere I don't want them to.

MOONPAD: Can I just ask you one more question?

INSTRUCTOR TENTION: No.

MOONPAD: Oh.

INSTRUCTOR TENTION: I got things to do. I got to run a dozen new rookies through stage-one flight training, get three officers through their advanced target-practice exams, make sure no one has electrified themselves with the buzz batons, and most important of all . . . have lunch.

MOONPAD: I understand.

INSTRUCTOR TENTION: You look kinda skinny, kid—you had lunch? You got money for lunch, right?

MOONPAD: Well . . .

[RECORDING ENDS][8]

[8] Editor's Note: Not that it's anyone else's business, BUT this is to confirm that even though he is just a totally unqualified intern with no experience whatsoever, Scratch Moonpad will be paid a full and fair wage for his contribution to this book. As soon as I make a profit, having deducted all my reasonable expenses, including, but not limited to, research, editing costs, travel, health insurance, membership in the Ancient Society of Tunneling Dwarfs, maintenance to my ex-wife, maintenance to my other ex-wife, grocery expenses, stinkworm pizza deliveries, entertaining costs, accommodation costs, accountancy fees, tab at the Second Skin nightclub, intern insurance, and veterinary costs, then I do solemnly declare and promise that Scratch Moonpad will receive 2.5 percent of all my profits beyond that. These to be paid twice a year on the winter and summer solstice, respectively, apart from years in which there is a lunar or solar eclipse on a weekend or a weekday, in which case no payment will be due.

GLOSSARY

AMAZON HELL CLAW	Large jungle-dwelling troll with a distinctive claw on both heels.
AMAZON TREE SPRITE	Subspecies of sprites adapted to gliding from tree to tree in a rain forest climate.
AMAZONIAN ELF	Fast-moving, tree-loving elves with blond hair and yellow arrowhead markings.
ANTARTIC BLUE	Species of troll able to stand extreme cold. Known for their huge size.
ATLANTIS	Domed underwater city. The second-largest fairy city in the Lower Elements.
ATLANTEAN PIXIE	Blue-skinned pixie from Atlantis.
BATTLE OF TAILLTE	Epic confrontation between the fairy races and the Mud People. Spoiler alert—we fairies lost and had to move underground.
BOOKE OF THE PEOPLE, THE	An ancient collection of fairy laws and rules.
BORRIS THE BLAGGER	Elfin writer of ancient texts of mostly dubious accuracy.
BUM PRINT	Like a fingerprint, but, you know, a bit more on the backside. Dwarfs claim each bum print is unique. So far no scientist has been willing to test this claim.
BUZZ BATONS	Weapon used by the L.E.P.

B'WA KELL	A dangerous goblin gang.
CENTAUR	One of the fairy races. The top half is humanoid to the waist, and the bottom half is that of a horse.
CENTAURIAN	The language of the centaur race. Believed to be the oldest form of writing in the world.
CROSS THE FLOOR	Term used to describe a gnome choosing to change from one house to another.
DARK SIDE OF THE MOON	The most powerful bottom burp a dwarf can do.
DEMON HIGH COUNCIL	Controlling organization of the demon race.
DRAGONFLY	Name of a set of outdated mechanical wings used by L.E.P. officers.
DWARF	Particularly good-looking and intelligent fairy race.[1]
DWARF GAS	Ugh. As bad as it sounds.
DWARF HAIR	Hair from a dwarf hardens when plucked and can be used to pick a lock.
DWARF PORE	Dwarf pores can take in water and enable a dwarf to climb up walls by acting as little suction cups.
ELF	Rather tall (for a fairy) and somewhat human looking, they are one of the most magical fairy races.
EXTINCTION	The wiping out of an entire race or species.
FIRE GNOMES	Brave gnomes from the Haven City fire department.
FLYING SQUAD	Aerial squad of L.E.P. officers.

[1] Editor's Note: In your heart you know it's true.

FOOTNOTE	An extra piece of information provided under the text.[2]
FROND	An elf who was the first king of the People. Also known as Frond the Easily Combustible.
GENERAL SCALENE	Well-known goblin general.
GIFT OF TONGUES	This magical fairy ability enables the user to speak and understand all languages.
GLOSSARY	A list of words and their meanings. This!
GOBLIN CORRECTIONAL FACILITY	Part of the Howler's Peak Prison.
GOBLIN TOWN	Area in Haven City populated mostly by goblins.
GOLDEN FIREBALL AWARD	Award given to the best piece of research into goblins in any given year.[3]
GREMLIN IN THE WORKS	Phrase used by Mud People for when something unexpectedly goes wrong with one of their machines.
GRUFF/SUSPECT ZERO	Believed to be the oldest troll in the world and responsible for sightings of what Mud People call the Yeti and Bigfoot.
HAVEN CITY	Fairy city hidden deep underground for protection against Mud People.
HEALING	Using magic to make better an illness or injury.
HOWLER'S PEAK	The prison facility of Haven City.
HUMMINGBIRD Z7	Name of a set of mechanical wings currently used by the L.E.P.

[2] Editor's Note: Like this.

[3] Editor's Note: Yeah, 'cus the world needs to know more about goblins.

HYBRID	A cross between two different species.
IMP	A young demon.
IMP SCHOOL	Educational establishment where imps are taught.
ISLAND OF HYBRAS	Home to the demon race. Originally part of the moon before being dislodged by a meteor and crashing to Earth.
JUMBO PIXIE	Larger-than-normal pixie. Usually thought to be due to the increased pressure in Atlantis.
KRAKEN	Large undersea creature the size of an island. Related to the People.
KRAKEN WATCH	Special department of the L.E.P. that observes krakens.
LADY HEATHERINGTON SMYTHE'S HEDGEROW	A romantic novel about the loves and bread baking of a nineteenth-century English aristocrat. Bizarrely the basis for a demon plan to conquer Mud People.
L.E.P.	The Lower Elements Police force.
L.E.P. ACADEMY	Training facility for L.E.P. cadets.
L.E.P.RECON	The division of the L.E.P. that deals with runaway or rogue fairies.
LYNGBAKR	Ancient Mud People name for a kraken.
MAGMA	Lava before it reaches the surface.
MAGMA POD	Small vessel built to withstand extreme heat and transport L.E.P. officers to the surface.
MESMER	A magic fairy power used to hypnotize Mud People.
METHANE	A strong-smelling explosive gas.

MIND-WIPE	A procedure that removes memories.
MUD PEOPLE	Violent and greedy life-forms that live on, and pollute, the surface of the planet.
NORD DIGGUMS	Expert tunneler, amazing editor, and possibly the greatest dwarf of all time. Also been known to provide glossaries on the side and in quick order. Let's talk.
ORANGE VENT TROLL	This troll lives deep down in the magma tunnels. Its hair has evolved into heat-resistant armor.
PEOPLE, THE	Name give to all the fairy races and different fairy species.
PIXEL	A cross between an elf and a pixie.
PIXIE	Highly intelligent, cunning fairy race. Less magical than elves.
POLICE PLAZA	Central location in Haven City and home to the L.E.P. Headquarters.
RIDGEBACK TROLL	Species of troll easily recognized by a ridge of thick hair running along its backbone.
RITUAL, THE	Ceremony to restore a fairy's magical powers. It requires the planting of a seed in moonlight.
RULE OF DWELLING	Ancient law causing any fairy who enters a Mud Person house without an invitation to become sick and lose their magical powers.
SACRED SCROLLS OF GLADFLY THE ANNOYING	Ancient text written by an annoying but reasonably truthful scribe.
SCROLLS OF CAPALLA	Ancient text written by centaurs.
SECOND SKIN NIGHTCLUB	A happy-times establishment frequented by goblins.

SECRET UNDERGROUND BROTHERHOOD OF DWARFS	The first rule of the Secret Underground Brotherhood of Dwarfs is you don't talk about the Secret Underground Brotherhood of Dwarfs.
SHELLY	The oldest known kraken in the world.[4]
SPRAY SPRITE	Subspecies of sprite adapted to life on ocean-facing cliffs with wings able to withstand strong ocean gusts.
SPRITE	Fairy race with natural wings and outstanding flying abilities.
STINKWORM	A small worm often cooked and served as a fairy delicacy.
SWAMP SPRITE	Adapted to life in the air *and* in the water.
TIME-STOP	Fairy spell to stop time in an area and separate it from the passage of real time.
TROLL RAMPAGE	A troll entirely out of control.
TROLL RIDER	A battlefield combination of a dwarf riding a semi-trained troll. Not witnessed in recent times.
WARLOCK	A member of a fairy race that has been trained and is skilled in the use of magic.
WATER SPRITE	A subspecies of sprite. Adapted for underwater life with gills and large sail-style wings.
WORLD WAR	Huge fight between different Mud People about which Mud Person owns which bit of mud aboveground. Nasty.
ZOO-TROLLOGY	The scientific study of trolls.

[4] Editor's Note: Probably.

BIBLIOGRAPHY

Alexandra, Professor Elizabeth, *Sticks and Carrots: A History of Centaurs*

Argon, Professor J., *Fowl and Fairy.*

Bane, Professor Wulf, *The Criminal Mastermind's Almanac*

Barbison, Carter Cooper, *Lady Heatherington Smythe's Hedgerow*

Beste, Dr. Belleva, *Shredding Skins: A New Look at Goblins*

Burniac, Lauren & Hesser, Elizabeth, *Still in the Dark: A History of Troll Humour*

Cuztard, Jac, *As Handsome as the Sea*

Day, Doodah, *Shellfish: Cooking Beyond the Law*

Fisher, Dr. W. G., *Atlantis: You're Never Alone in a Dome*

Fishlicker, Dr. Wight, *The Terror of the Trolls* (published posthumously)

Fleetstream, T. J., *Join In! Techniques for the Social Inclusion of the Socially Excluded*

Fogelman, Dr. Ronald Howard, *Battle: The Hill of Taillte*

Francis, Dr. V. J. *The Life and Crimes of Gentleman George*

Gruff, Billy Goat, *Bridge: My Test and My Triumph*

Higgins, Dr. John, *Strokes of Genius: Hervé's The Fairy Thief*

McTortoor, Grazen, *The Making of "Troll Sundown"*

Oot, Professor Seekem, *My Life with Trolls*

Tention, Paye, *My Way or the Highway*

Valentine, Widget, *Stinkworms Have Feelings Too!*

Verbil, Chix, *The High Life: My Time on the Wing*

Wall, Matt, *Cave-In: Captain Eusebius Fowl and the Saga of the HMS Octagon*

ACKNOWLEDGMENT

A VERY BIG THANK-YOU TO MR. COLFER FOR ALLOWING US TO PLAY IN HIS MOST MAGICAL TOY BOX.

GONZALO KENNY was born in Buenos Aires, Argentina, in 1979. From an early age he was interested in art and drawing. And he has always had a fascination for science fiction, horror, and fantastic universes. His passion led him to an art school, and later to University, where he completed a degree as an Industrial Designer. And eventually, he followed his dream and became an illustrator of epic fantasy books.

For years, he has collaborated with author Liliana Bodoc in the visual development of *La Saga de los Confines*—one of the most renowned epic-fantasy novels in Latin America.

Currently, Gonzalo is working as a freelance artist for the global publishing market. His illustrations of fantasy art and conceptual design are published in board games, videogames, trading cards, and in the entertainment and film industry.

PHOTO BY GIOVANNI RIGANO

ANDREW DONKIN is a writer and graphic novelist. He is a longtime collaborator with Eoin Colfer and the pair recently co-authored the award-winning original graphic novel *Illegal*, with art by Giovanni Rigano. The terrific trio have also turned the first four Artemis Fowl books featuring everyone's favorite criminal mastermind into best-selling, award-winning, graphic novel adaptations.

Andrew has written over seventy books including children's books, graphic novels, and even the odd book for grown-ups. His work has been translated into over twenty languages and has sold over nine million copies around the world. He lives near the river Thames in London with his partner and their two children. Find him at www.andrewdonkin.com and on Twitter and Instagram @andrewdonkin.